CLAIMING MY
HIDDEN SON

CLAIMING MY HIDDEN SON

MAYA BLAKE

MILLS & BOON

First published in Great Britain 2019
by Mills & Boon, an imprint of HarperCollins*Publishers*
1 London Bridge Street, London, SE1 9GF

Large Print edition 2020

© 2019 Maya Blake

ISBN: 978-0-263-08426-9

MIX
Paper from
responsible sources
FSC **FSC® C007454**

This book is produced from independently certified FSC™ paper to ensure responsible forest management. For more information visit www.harpercollins.co.uk/green.

Printed and bound in Great Britain
by CPI Group (UK) Ltd, Croydon, CR0 4YY

PROLOGUE

THE DRUMMING IN my ears was loud. So loud I had the fleeting thought that I was on the verge of suffering a stroke. Of doing myself irreparable harm and comprehensively ending this debacle once and for all.

But that would be too easy.

And the headline…

I could see it now.

Axios Xenakis Suffers Stroke Due to Family Pressures!

They would have no clue as to the unreasonable part, of course. Despite the media outlets lauding the story of the Xenakis near-ruin to phenomenal rise on a regular basis these days, they would be swift to jump on past flaws. Old skeletons would be dragged out of closets. I would be deemed weak. Broken. Not quite up to the task of managing a global conglomerate.

Just like my father.

Just as my grandfather had been falsely labelled after that one risky move that had seen all his hard work whittled away to almost nothing.

He'd had to bear that one misfortune all the way to his grave.

Once a titan of his industry, a simple decision to align himself with the wrong partner had decimated him, leaving the Xenakis name with a stench of failure that had lingered long after his death, causing insidious damage.

Damage that had taken back-breaking hard work to reverse, with my refusal to allow my family name to sink without a trace spurring me to seek daring solutions.

The Xenakis name was no longer one to be ashamed of. Now it was synonymous with success and innovation—a global conglomerate that *Fortune 500* companies vied to be associated with.

However, the solution being proposed to me now was one set to resurrect the unsavoury ghosts of the past, with their talons of barefaced greed—

'Ax, are you listening? Did you hear what Father said?' asked Neo, my brother.

'Of course I heard it. I'm not deaf,' I replied, with more than a snap to my voice.

'Thank God for that—although you do a great stone statue impression.'

I ignored Neo and fixed my gaze on the man seated behind the large antique desk. My father was studying me with a mixture of regret and apprehension. He knew my precise thoughts on the subject being discussed.

No, not *discussed*.

It was being *thrust* upon me.

'No,' I replied firmly. 'There has to be another way.'

The tension in the room elevated, but this was too serious for me to mince my words. Too serious to let the elephant that always loomed in the room on occasions like this cloud my judgement.

I simply couldn't allow the fact that my grandfather had chosen me as his successor instead of my father to get in the way of this discussion. Nor could I allow the resentment and guilt that had always tainted my relationship with my father to alter my view on what was being proposed.

What was done was done. I'd turned the tides and restored the fortunes of my family. For that even my father couldn't object.

Which was why I was a little surprised when he emphatically shook his head.

'There isn't. Your grandfather was of sound mind when he made the arrangement.'

'Even though he was judged otherwise in other areas?'

Barely fettered bitterness filtered through my

voice. The injustices dealt to my grandfather and mentor, the man who taught me everything I know, still burned like acid all these years after his untimely death.

'Now is not the time to reopen old wounds, Axios,' my father said, jaw clenched.

My quiet fury burned even as I accepted his words. 'I agree. Now is the time to discuss ways to get me *out* of this nonsense.'

And it *was* nonsense to expect an arrangement like this to hold water.

'A sweeping agreement where the other party gets to call the shots whenever they like? How come the lawyers haven't ripped this to shreds?' I demanded, striving to keep a tighter rein on my ire.

My father's lips firmed. 'I've spent the last month discussing it with our counsel. We can fight it in court, and probably win, but it'll be a protracted affair. And is now really the time to draw adverse publicity to the company? Or drag your grandfather's name through the mud again for that matter?'

My own lips flattened as again I grimly accepted he was right. With Xenakis Aeronautics poised for its biggest global expansion yet, the timing was far from ideal.

Which was exactly what Yiannis Petras had banked on.

'You mentioned you'd offered him ten million euros and he refused? Let's double the offer,' I suggested.

Neo shook his head. 'I already tried. Petras is hell-bent on Option A or Option B.'

The breath left my lungs in a rush. 'Over my dead body will I go for Option A and hand over twenty-five percent of Xenakis Aeronautics,' I replied coldly. 'Not for the paltry quarter of a million his father bailed Grandpapa out with, while almost crippling him with steep interest repayments!'

The company I'd spent gruelling years saving was now worth several billion euros.

My brother shrugged. 'Then it's Option B. A full and final one hundred million euros, plus marriage to his daughter for minimum term of one year.'

A cold shudder tiptoed down my spine.

Marriage.

To a bride I didn't want and with a connection to a family that had brought mine nothing but misery, pain and near destitution.

During the formative years of my life I witnessed how a fall from grace could turn family members against each other. Clawing my own family out of that quagmire while other factions sneered and expected me to fail had opened my eyes to the true nature of relationships.

Outwardly, the Xenakis were deemed a strong unit now, but the backbiting had never gone away. The barely veiled expectation that everything I'd achieved would be brought down like a pile of loose bricks and that history would repeat itself was a silent challenge I rose to each morning.

While my extended family now enjoyed the fruits of my labour, and even tripped over themselves to remain in my good graces, deep down I knew a simple misstep was all it would take for their frivolous loyalties to falter.

I didn't even blame them.

How could I when my own personal interactions had repeatedly taken the same route? Each liaison I entered into eventually devolved into a disillusioning level of avarice and status-grabbing.

It was why my relationships now had a strict time limit of weeks. A few months, tops. Which made the thought of tying myself to one woman for twelve long months simply…*unthinkable*.

My chest tightened, and the urge to rail at my grandfather for putting me in this position seared me with shame before I suppressed it.

He'd been in an equally impossible position. I knew first-hand what the toll of keeping his family together had cost him—had watched deep grooves etch his grey face once vibrant with laughter and seen his shoulders slump under the heavy burden of loss.

Yes, he should have told me about this Sword of Damocles hanging over my head. But he was gone. Thanks to the ruthless greed of the Petras family. A family hell-bent on extracting another pound of flesh they didn't deserve.

'The hundred million I understand. But why insist on marriage to the daughter?' I asked my brother as his words pierced the fog of my thoughts.

Neo shrugged again. 'Who knows how men like Petras think? Maybe he just wants to offload her. The clout that comes from marrying into the Xenakis family isn't without its benefits,' he mused.

I shuddered, the reminder that, to most people, my family and I were nothing but meal tickets sending a shock of bitterness through me.

'And did you meet this woman I'm to tie myself to?'

He nodded. 'She's...' He stopped and smiled slyly. 'I'll let you judge for yourself.' His gaze left mine to travel over my grey pinstriped suit. 'But I'm thinking you two will hit it off.'

Before I could demand an explanation my father leaned forward. 'Enough, Neo.' My father's gaze swung to me, steel reflected in his eyes. 'We can't delay any longer. Yiannis Petras wants an answer by morning.'

The pressure gripping my nape escalated— the effect of the noose closing round it ramping up my discord. Marriage was the last thing I wanted. To anyone. But especially to a Petras. Both my grandparents and my parents had been strained to breaking point because of the Petras family's actions, with ill-health borne of worry taking my grandmother before her time too.

There had to be another way...

'What's her name?' I asked my father—not because I cared but because I needed another moment to think. To wrap my head around this insanity.

'Calypso Athena Petras. But I believe she responds to Callie.'

Beside me, Neo smirked again. 'A dramatic name for a dramatic situation!'

I balled my fist and attempted to breathe through the churning in my gut. First they'd forced my grandfather's business into the ground, until he'd broken his family right down the middle by working himself into an early grave. Now this…

'Show me the agreement.' I needed to see it for myself, find a way to assimilate what I'd been committed to.

My father slid the document across the desk. I read it, my fingers clenching as with each paragraph the noose tightened.

Twelve months of my life, starting from the exchange of vows, after which either party would be free to divorce.

Twelve months during which the Petras family who, by a quirk of karma—if you believe in that sort of thing—had fallen on even harder times than they'd condemned my family to would be free to capitalise fully on their new status of wealth and privilege by association.

My lips twisted. I intended to have my lawyers draft divorce papers before I went anywhere near a church.

I exhaled, knowing my subconscious had already accepted the situation.

'Don't overthink it, brother. You're thirty-three next month. This will be over by your thirty-fourth birthday. If you bite the bullet,' Neo offered helpfully.

Slowly, I dragged myself back under control. 'I've worked too hard and too long to restore our family back to where it belongs to lose it to a greedy opportunist. If there's no other way… tell Petras we have a deal.'

My father nodded, relieved, before he sent me another nervous glance. The kind that announced there was something more equally unsavoury to deliver.

'What now?' My patience was hanging by a thread.

'Besides paying for the wedding, we also need to present the family with a…a dowry of sorts. Petras has asked for Kosima.'

I surged to my feet, uncaring that my chair tipped over. '*Excuse* me?'

My father's face tightened. 'No one has stepped foot on the island since your grandfather passed—'

'That doesn't mean I want to hand it over to the son of the man who caused his death!'

A flash of pain dimmed his eyes. 'We don't know that to be strictly true.'

'Don't we? Did you not see for yourself the pressure he was under? He only started drinking after the problems with Petras started. Is it any wonder his heart failed?'

'Easy, brother,' Neo urged. 'Father is right. The house is rotting away and the land around it is nothing but a pile of weeds and stones.'

But I was beyond reason. Beyond furious at this last damning request.

'Grandpapa loved that island. It belongs to us. I'm not going to hand it over to Petras. Isn't it enough that he's imposing this bilious arrangement on us?'

'Is it enough for you to drag your heels on this last hurdle?' My father parried.

Unable to remain still, I strode to the window of the building that housed the headquarters of Xenakis Aeronautics, the global airline empire I'd headed for almost a decade. For a full minute I watched traffic move back and forth on the busy Athens streets while I grappled with this last condition.

I sensed my brother and father approach. I didn't acknowledge them as they positioned themselves on either side of me and waited.

Waited for the only response that I could conceivably give. The words burned in my throat. Left a trail of ash on my tongue. But it had to be done. I had to honour my grandfather's request, no matter my personal view on it. Or I'd risk everything he'd built. Risk mocking the sacrifice that had taken the ultimate toll.

'Tell Petras he has a deal.'

My father's hand arrived on my shoulder in silent gratitude, after which he exited quietly.

Neo chose more exuberant congratulations, but even then I barely felt him slap my shoulder.

'Think of it this way. For twelve months you'll be free of all the scheming socialites and su-permodels who've been falling over themselves to extract a commitment from you. I'll happily carry that burden for you instead.'

'Unless you wish to date one of those super-models whilst sporting a black eye, I suggest you leave my office immediately,' I growled.

My brother's laughter echoed in my ears long after he'd slammed the door behind him.

But long before the echo died I made another silent vow to myself. Petras and his kin would pay for what they'd done to my family. Before the stipulated year of marriage was out they'd regret tangling with the Xenakis family.

CHAPTER ONE

'SMILE, CALYPSO. IT'S the happiest day of your life!'

'Here, let me put some more blusher on your cheeks...you're so pale. Perhaps a bit more shadow for your beautiful eyes...'

Beneath the endless layers of white tulle that some faceless stranger had deemed the perfect wedding gown material and gone to town with my fingers bunched into fists. When the tight clenches didn't help, I bit the tip of my tongue and fought the urge to scream.

But I was past hysteria. *That* unfortunate state had occurred two weeks prior, when my father had informed me just how he'd mapped out the rest of my life. How it was my turn to help restore our family's honour.

Or else.

The cold shivers racing up and down my spine had become familiar in the last month, after a few days spent in denial that my father would truly carry out his intentions.

I'd quickly accepted that he would.

Years of bitterness and humiliation and failure

to emulate his ruthless father's dubious acclaim had pushed him over the edge once and for all.

The soft bristles of the blusher brush passed feverishly over my cheeks. The make-up artist determined to transform me into an eager, blushing, starry-eyed bride.

But I was far from eager and a million miles away from starry-eyed.

The only thing they'd got right in this miserable spectacle was the virginal white.

If I'd had a choice that too would have been a lie. At twenty-four I knew, even in my sheltered existence, that being a virgin was a rare phenomenon. At least now I realised why my father had been hell-bent on thwarting my every encounter with the opposite sex. Why he'd ruthlessly vetted my friendships, curtailed my freedom.

I'd believed my choices had been so abruptly limited since the moment my mother fell from grace. Since she returned home the broken prodigal wife and handed my father all the weapons he needed to transform himself from moderately intolerable to fearsome tyrant. I thought I'd been swept along by the merciless broom of wronged party justice, but he'd had a completely different purpose for me.

A purpose which had brought me to this moment.

My wedding day.

The next shudder coagulated in my chin, making it wobble like jelly before I could wrestle my composure back under control.

Luckily the trio of women who'd descended on our house twenty-four hours ago were clucking about pre-wedding nerves, then clucking some more about how understandable my fraught emotions were, considering who my prospective husband was.

Axios Xenakis.

A man I'd never met.

Sure, like everyone in Greece I knew who he was. A wildly successful airline magnate worth billions and head of the influential Xenakis family. A family whose ill fortune, unlike mine, had been reversed due the daring innovation of its young CEO.

It was rumoured that Axios Xenakis was the kind of individual whose projections could cause stock markets to rise or fall. The various articles I'd read about him had boggled my mind—the idea that any one person could wield such power and authority was bewildering. To top it off, Axios Xenakis was drop-dead gorgeous, if a little fierce-looking.

Everything about the man was way too visceral and invasive. Just a simple glance at his image online had evoked the notion that he could see into my soul, glean my deepest desires and use them against me. It was probably why he was often seen in the company of sophisticated heiresses and equally influential A-listers.

Which begged the question—why the Petras family? More specifically, why *me*?

What did a man who dated socialites and heiresses on a regular basis, as was thoroughly documented in the media, have to gain by shackling himself to me?

I knew it had something to do with the supreme smugness my father had been exhibiting in the last several weeks but he had refused to disclose. Somehow, behind the sneers and bitterness whenever the Xenakis name came up over the years, my father had been scheming. And that scheming had included me.

In all my daydreams about attaining my freedom, marriage hadn't featured anywhere. I wanted the freedom to dictate who I socialised with, what I ate, the pleasure to paint my watercolours without fear of recrimination, without judgement… The freedom to live life on *my* terms.

The hope of one day achieving those things had stopped me from succumbing to abject misery.

But not like *this*!

I forced my gaze to the mirror and promptly looked away again. My eyes were desolate pools, my cheeks artificially pink with excess rouge. My lips were turned down, reflecting my despair since learning that I was promised to a stranger. One who'd demanded a wedding within twenty-eight days.

My flat refusal had merely garnered a cold shrug from my father, before he had gone for the jugular—my one weakness.

My mother.

As if summoned by my inner turmoil, the electric whine of a wheelchair disturbed the excited chatter of the stylists. The moment they realised the mother of the bride had entered the bedroom, their attention shifted to her.

Taking advantage of the reprieve, I surreptitiously rubbed at my cheeks with a tissue, removing a layer of blusher. The icy peach lipstick disappeared with the second swipe across my lips, leaving me even paler than before but thankfully looking less of a lost, wide-eyed freak. Quickly hanging the thick lace veil over my face to hide the alteration, I stood and turned, watching as the women fawned over my mother.

Iona Petras had been stunningly beautiful once upon a time. Growing up, I was in awe of her statuesque beauty, her vivacity and sheer joy for life. Her laughter had lit up my day, her intelligence and love of the arts fuelling my own appreciation for music and painting.

Now, greying and confined, she was still a beautiful woman. But along with her broken body had come a broken spirit no amount of pretending or smiling, or even gaining the elevated position as mother of the bride, soon to marry a man most deemed a demigod, could disguise.

She withstood the stylists' ministrations without complaint, her half-hearted smile only slipping when her eyes met mine. Within them I saw ravaging misery and the sort of unending despair that came with the life sentence she'd imposed on herself by returning when she should have fled.

But, just as I'd had to remain here because of her, I knew my mother had returned home because of me. And somewhere along the line Iona Petras had accepted her fate.

'Leave us, please,' she said to the stylists, her voice surprisingly steely.

The women withdrew. She wheeled herself closer, her face pinched with worry. For the longest minute she stared at me.

'Are you all right?'

I tensed, momentarily panicked that she'd learned what I'd hidden from her for the last few weeks. As much as I'd tried to ignore the ever-growing pain in my abdomen, I couldn't any more. Not only had it become a constant dull ache, it had become a reminder that even health-wise my life wasn't my own. That I might well be succumbing to the very real ailment that had taken my grandmother—

'Callie? Are you ready?'

Realising she was talking about the wedding ceremony, I felt the urge to succumb to hysteria pummel me once again. As did the fierce need to be selfish just this once…to simply flee and let the chips fall where they may.

'Is anyone ever ready to marry a man they've never met?' I asked. 'Please tell me you've found out why he's demanding I do this?' I pleaded.

Eyes a shade darker than my own lapis-lazuli-coloured ones turned mournful as she shook her head. 'No. Your father still refuses to tell me. My guess is that it has something to do with your grandfather and old man Xenakis.' Before I could ask what she meant, she continued, 'Any-way, Yiannis will be looking for me, so I need to be quick.'

She reached inside the stylish designer jacket that matched her lavender gown and produced a thick cream envelope, her fingers shaking as she stared at it.

'What's that?' I asked when she made no move to speak.

Within her gaze came a spark of determination I hadn't seen in years. My heart leapt into my throat as she caught my hand in hers and squeezed it tight.

'My sweet Callie, I know I've brought misery to your life with my actions—'

'No, Mama, you haven't. I promise,' I countered firmly.

She stared at me. 'I'm not sure whether to be proud or to admonish you for being such a good liar. But I know what I've done. My selfishness has locked you in this prison with me when you should be free to pursue what young girls your age ought to be doing.' Her fingers tightened on mine. 'I want you to make me a promise,' she pleaded, her voice husky with unshed tears.

I nodded because…what else could I do? 'Anything you want, Mama.'

She held out the envelope. 'Take this. Hide it in the safest place you can.'

I took it, frowning at the old-fashioned cursive lettering spelling out my name. 'What's this?'

'It's from your grandmother.'

'Yiayia Helena?' A tide of sorrow momentarily washed over me, my heart still missing the grandmother I'd lost a year ago.

My mother nodded. 'She said I'd know when you needed it. And even if I'm wrong…'

She paused, a faraway look in her eyes hinting that she was indulging in all those might-have-beens that sparked my own desperate imagination. When she refocused, her gaze moved dully over my wedding dress.

'Even if this…alliance turns out to be tolerable, it'll help to know you were loved by your grandmother. That should you need her she'll be there for you the way I wasn't.'

I held on tighter to her hand. 'I know you love me, Mama.'

She shook her head, tears brimming her eyes. 'Not the way a mother should love her child, without selfish intentions that end up harming her. I took the wrong turn with you. I left you alone with your father when I should have taken you with me. Maybe if I had—' She stopped, took a deep breath and dabbed at her tears before braving my worried stare again. 'All I ask is that you find a way to forgive me one day.'

'Mama—' I stopped when she gave a wrenching sob.

Her gaze dropped to the envelope in my hand. 'Hang on to that, Callie. And don't hesitate to use it when you need it. Promise me,' she insisted fervently.'

'I... I promise.'

She sniffed, nodded, then abruptly turned the wheelchair and manoeuvred herself out of my bedroom.

Before I could process our conversation I was again surrounded by mindless chatter, unable to breathe or think. The only solid thing in my world became the envelope I clutched tightly in my hand. And when I found that within the endless folds of tulle the designer had fashioned a pocket, I nearly cried with relief as I slipped the envelope into it.

Even without knowing its contents, just knowing it came from my grandmother—the woman who'd helped me stand up to my father's wrath more times than I could count, who'd loved and reassured me on a daily basis during my mother's year-long absence when I was fifteen years old—kept me from crumbling as my father arrived and with a brisk nod offered his stiff arm, ordered me to straighten my spine...and escorted me to my fate.

The chapel was filled to the brim, according to the excited chatter of the household staff, and as my father led me out to a flower-bedecked horse-drawn carriage I got the first indication of what was to come.

Over the last three weeks I'd watched with a sense of surrealism as construction crews and landscapers descended on our little corner of the world to transform the church and surrounding area from a place of rundown dilapidation into its former whitewashed charming glory.

The usually quiet streets of Nicrete, a sleepy village in the south of the island of Skyros, the place generations of the Petras family had called home, buzzed with fashionably dressed strangers—all guests of Axios Xenakis. With the main means of getting on and off the island being by boat, the harbour had become a place of interest in the last few days.

Every hotel and guest house on the island was booked solid. Expensive speedboats and a handful of super-yachts had appeared on the horizon overnight, and now bobbed in the Aegean beneath resplendent sunshine.

Of course the man I was to marry chose to do things differently.

My carriage was halfway between home and the church when the loud, mechanical whine of powerful rotors churned the air. Children shouted in excitement and raced towards the hilltop as three sleek-looking helicopters flew overhead to settle on the newly manicured lawns of the park usually used as recreational grounds for families. Today the whole park had been cordoned off— evidently to receive these helicopters.

Beneath the veil I allowed myself a distasteful moue. But the barrier wasn't enough to hide my father's smug smile as he watched the helicopters. Or his nod of satisfaction as several distinguished-looking men and designer-clad women alighted from the craft.

I averted my face, hoping the ache in my heart and the pain in my belly wouldn't manifest itself in the hysteria I'd been trying to suppress for what seemed like for ever. But I couldn't prevent the words from tumbling from my lips.

'It's not too late, Papa. Whatever this is… Perhaps if you told me why, we can find a way—'

'I have already found a way, child.'

'Don't call me a child—I'm twenty-four years old!'

That pulse of rebellion, which I'd never quite been able to curb, eagerly fanned by Yiayia when she was alive, slipped its leash. She'd never got on well with my father, and in a way standing up to him now, despite the potential fallout for my mother, felt like honouring her memory.

His eyes narrowed. 'If you wanted to help then you should've taken that business degree at university, instead of the useless arts degree you're saddled with.'

'I told you—I'm not interested in a corporate career.'

Nor was I interested in being constantly reminded that I wasn't the son he'd yearned for. The one he'd hoped would help him save Petras Industries, the family company which now teetered on the brink of bankruptcy.

'*Ne*—and just like your mother you let me down. Once again it has fallen to *me* to find a way. And I have. So now you will smile and do your duty by this family. You will say your vows and marry Xenakis.'

I bit my lip at this reminder of yet another bone of contention between us. I'd fought hard for the right to leave the island to pursue my arts degree, only returning because of my mother. The small art gallery I worked at part-time on Nicrete was a way of keeping my sanity, even as I mourned my wasted degree.

'After that, what then?'

He shrugged. 'After that you will belong to him. But remember that regardless of the new name you're taking on you're still a Petras. If you do anything to bring the family into disrepute you will bear the consequences.'

My heart lurched, my fists balling in pain and

frustration—because I knew exactly what my father meant.

The *consequences* being my father's ability to manipulate my mother's guilt and ensure maximum suffering. His constant threats to toss her out with only the clothes on her back, to abandon her to her fate the way she'd briefly abandoned her family. But while my mother had deserted her child and marriage in the name of a doomed love, my father was operating from a place of pure revenge. To him, his wife had humiliated and betrayed him, and he was determined to repay her by keeping her prisoner. Ensuring that at every waking moment she was reminded of her fall from grace and his power over her.

The reason that I'd been roped in as a means to that end was my love for my mother.

Eight years ago, when he'd returned home with my absentee mother after the doctors in Athens had called and informed him that she'd been in a crash, and that the man she'd run away with was dead, he'd laid out new family rules. My mother would stay married to him. She would become a dutiful wife and mother, doing everything in her power to not bring another speck of disgrace to the family. In return he would ensure her medical needs were met, and that she would be given the finest treatment to adjust to her new wheel-chair-bound life.

For my part, I would act the devoted daughter...or my mother would suffer.

The horses whinnying as they came to a stop at the steps leading to the church doors dragged me to the present, pushing my heartache aside and replacing it with apprehension.

The last of the guests were entering while organ music piped portentously in the air. In less than an hour I would be married to a man I'd never exchanged a single word with. A man who had somehow fallen in league with my father for reasons I still didn't know.

I glanced at my father, desperate to ask why. His stony profile warned me not to push my luck. Like my heartache, I smothered my rebellion.

My father stepped out of the carriage and held out his hand. Mine shook, and again I was glad for the veil's cover to hide my tear-prickled eyes.

A small part of me was grateful that my father didn't seem in a hurry to march me down the aisle because he was basking in the lime-light that momentarily banished the shadow of scandal and humiliation he'd lived under for the past eight years. For once people weren't talking about his wife's infidelity. Or the fact that the woman who'd deserted him had returned in a wheelchair. Or that he'd taken her back just so he could keep her firmly under his thumb in retribution.

Today he was simply the man who'd seemingly bagged one of the most eligible bachelors in the world for his daughter—not the once illustrious but now downtrodden businessman who'd lost the Petras fortune his father had left him.

The doors to the church yawned open, ready to receive their unwilling sacrifice. My footsteps faltered and my father sent me a sharp look. Unable to meet his eyes without setting off the spark of mutiny attempting to rekindle itself inside me, I kept my gaze straight.

I needed to do this for my mother.

I spotted her in the front row, her head held high despite her fate, and it lent me the strength to put one foot in front of the other. The slight weight of my grandmother's envelope in my pocket helped me ignore the rabid curiosity and speculative whispers of three hundred strangers.

Unfortunately there was only one place left to look. At the towering figure of the man waiting in perfect stillness facing the altar.

He didn't twitch nor fidget. Didn't display any outward signs of being a nervous groom.

His broad back and wide shoulders seemed to

go on for ever, and his proud head and unyielding stance announced his power and authority. He didn't speak to the equally tall, commanding figure next to him, as most grooms did with their best man. In fact both men stood as if to military attention, their stance unwavering.

My gaze flicked away from Axios Xenakis, my breath stalling in my throat the closer I approached. Even without seeing his face I sensed a formidable aura—one that forced me again to wonder why he was doing this. What did he have to gain with this alliance?

He could have any woman he wanted. So why me?

And why had several butterflies suddenly taken flight within my belly?

Wild instinct urged me to fan my rebellion to life. *Fight or flight.* Pick one and deal with the consequences later.

But even as the thoughts formed they were discarded.

I had no choice. None whatsoever.

But maybe this man I was marrying would be a little more malleable than my father. Maybe—

He turned. And the feeble little hope died a horrible death.

Eyes the colour of polished gunmetal bored

into me as if they were with fierce, merciless hooks. They probed beneath the veil with such force that for a moment I imagined I was naked—that he could see my every weakness and flaw, see to the heart of my deepest desire for freedom.

His lips were pressed into a formidable line, his whole demeanour austere. Axios Xenakis could have been in a boardroom, preparing to strike a deal to make himself another billion euros, not poised before an altar, about to commit himself to a wife he'd never met.

I catalogued his breathtaking features. Wondered if that rugged boxer's jaw ever relaxed—whether the cut-glass sharpness of his cheekbones ever softened in a smile. Did he maintain constant control of those sleek eyebrows so they were permanently brooding? Did his nose ever wrinkle in laughter?

Why was I interested?

I was nothing but part of a transaction to him—one he didn't seem entirely thrilled about, judging by his icy regard. So it didn't matter that the olive vibrancy of his skin drew from me more than a fleeting look, or that he was without a doubt the most strikingly handsome man I'd ever seen.

He was a world removed from the boys I'd

sneakily dated at university, before my father had found out and ruthlessly thwarted my chances with them before anything resembling a relationship could form.

Axios Xenakis belonged in a stratosphere of his own. One I was apprehensive about inhabiting.

My footsteps stalled and I heard my father's sharp intake of breath. It was swiftly followed by the tight grip of his hand in warning.

Don't disgrace the family.

Defiance sparked again.

But then I saw my mother's head turn. The ubiquitous misery filmed her eyes, but alongside it was a look so fierce it might have been a reflection from my grandmother's eyes.

It was a look that infused me with courage.

It's up to you, it said. *Do this...or don't.*

My heart thundered. The need to turn around and simply walk away was a wild cyclone churning through me.

At the altar, Axios's eyes never shifted from me, his stance unchanging in the face of my clear reluctance. It was as if he knew what I'd decide and was simply waiting me out.

And, since I was playing in a game whose rules no one had bothered to apprise me of, there was only one move I could make.

I would play this round, then fight my corner later.

With that firm promise echoing inside me, I stepped up to the altar.

I saw a fleeting disappointment in his eyes before he masked his features. He was *disappointed*? Did that mean he didn't want this?

Wild hope flared within me even as bewilderment mounted. If he didn't want this then there might be room to negotiate. Room to get what I wanted out of this.

Realising I was staring, and that my father had been dispatched and I was now the sole focus of Axios Xenakis' eyes, I hurriedly averted my gaze. But not before acknowledging that up close he was even more electrifying. Perhaps it was the severity of his grey suit. Or the fact that the hand he held out to me screamed a silent command.

The last strains of the hymn trailed away, leaving behind a charged silence. With each second it weighed heavier, pressing down on me.

His hand extended another inch, and heavy expectation thickened the air.

With a deep breath, inevitably I slipped my hand into his—and joined the stranger who was to be my husband.

Almost immediately he released me. But the sensation of his touch lingered, and a sizzling chain reaction I was unprepared for travelled up my arm, flaring wide.

It was enough momentarily to drown out the intonation of the priest's voice as he began the ceremony.

I rallied long enough to murmur the words I'd reluctantly memorised and, when the time came, to pick up the larger of the two platinum wedding bands.

With fingers that still trembled I faced Axios. The impact of his eyes, his towering frame, the much too handsome face momentarily erased the words from my brain.

In silence he held out his left hand, his laser eyes boring into me as he simply...*waited*.

'I take thee...'

'For better or worse...'

'With my body...'

'Love, honour, cherish...'

'Till death...'

With each spoken vow my heart squeezed tighter, the mechanical delivery I'd expected to give morphing into a whispered outpouring wrapped in consternation.

The second I was done he reached for the other

ring without taking his eyes off me, again holding out his hand for mine.

And then Axios Xenakis spoke for the first time.

'I, Axios Xenakis, take thee, Calypso Athena Petras...'

The rest of his words were lost to me as the deep, hypnotic cadence of his voice struck like Zeus's thunderbolt into a place I didn't even know existed until that moment.

His voice was...*sexy*. Alluring. Magnetic.

It seemed impossible that a voice could be all those things, and yet I felt every one.

The cold brush of platinum on my skin brought me back to myself just in time to hear the priest announce us as man and wife. To say that my new husband could now kiss me.

I started to turn away. Because this was a far cry from a normal wedding ceremony. And we were far removed from two people in love.

Large, firm hands cupped my shoulders, shocking me into stillness. Unable to stop a cascade of light shivers, I held my breath as he lifted the heavy veil and draped it behind me with unhurried movements. I watched his gaze take in my bound hair, the small headband made of tiny diamonds and pearls that had belonged to Yiayia

Helena and the similar necklace adorning my throat.

Had he been anyone else I might have entertained the notion that Axios Xenakis was reluctant to look into the face of the woman he'd just committed himself to. Because when his piercing grey eyes finally settled on me, I caught a momentary confusion, then his eyes widened and his jaw slackened for a split second before he reasserted supreme control.

Any fleeting pleasure I'd felt at gaining some unknown upper hand fled as heat suffused my face at his intense, almost shocked scrutiny.

Admitting that I should have left the make-up artist's work alone didn't help my urge to squirm under his candid regard. But I forced myself to hold his gaze, ignore the consternation in his eyes and the humiliating thud of my heartbeat.

Just when I thought he intended to drag the torture out for ever he slid one finger beneath my chin to nudge my head upward. Caught in the mysterious hypnosis of his gaze, I watched his head descend, so close that heat from his skin singed mine.

I braced myself, my stomach churning with emotions I couldn't name.

I'd been kissed before. Those university colleagues I'd toyed with before my father's bitter reach had scared them away. None of them had elicited this level of shivery anticipation.

His kiss arrived, subtle as a butterfly's wing and powerful as a sledgehammer. Sensation rocked through me like an earthquake, dizzying and terrifying, leaving me with nothing to do but to brace my hands on his chest, anchor myself to reality somehow.

But all that did was compound my situation. Because the solid wall of his chest was like sculpted warm steel, inviting the kind of exploration that had no place in this time and space.

Pull away.

Before I could, he gave a sharp intake of breath. In the next moment I was free of him and he was turning away.

Back to earth with a shaky thud, I fought angry bewilderment even as I strove for composure before our three-hundred-strong audience.

The feeling lingered all through our walk down the aisle, through our stiff poses for pictures and then the ride back up the hill to the crumbling mansion overlooking the harbour— the only home I'd ever known.

The horse and carriage had been swapped for a sleek limousine with darkened windows and a partition that ensured privacy. Beside me Axios maintained a stony silence, one I wasn't inclined to break despite the dark, enigmatic looks he slanted me every now and then.

When it all became too much, I snatched in a breath and faced him. 'Is there something on your mind?'

One eyebrow quirked. 'As conversations go, that's not quite what I expected as our first. But then I'm making many surprising discoveries.'

He wasn't the only one! 'What's that supposed to mean?'

He didn't reply immediately. Then, 'You're not what I was led to expect.'

I couldn't help my lips twisting. 'You are aware of how absurd that sounds, aren't you?'

He stiffened, and I got the notion that once again something about me had surprised him. 'No. Enlighten me,' he replied dryly.

'Not what you were *led to expect*?' The slight screech in my voice warned me that hysteria might be winning but I couldn't stop. 'Let me guess—you thought you were getting some biddable wallflower who would tremble and trip over herself to please you?'

You were trembling minutes ago, when he kissed you.

I ignored the voice and met his gaze.

He'd turned into a pillar of stone. 'Considering the ink isn't dry on our marriage certificate, perhaps we should strive not to have our first disagreement. Unless you wish to break some sort of record?' he rasped, gunmetal eyes boring into me.

Apart from our marriage, I still didn't know the precise details of the deal between my father and my new husband and it momentarily stalled my response. But the fire burning inside me wouldn't be doused.

'I get the feeling you're just as...*invested* in this thing as my father is, so it bears repeating that you're *not* getting a simpering lackey who will jump through hoops to amuse you.'

His eyes narrowed. 'Your *father*? Not you?'

Short of revealing my ignorance on the matter, I had to prevaricate. 'I'm a Petras—same as he.'

Something that looked very much like contempt flickered through his eyes. 'Consider me forewarned,' he replied cryptically.

Before I could query what he meant the limo was pulling up to the double doors of my family home. Liveried footmen hurried to throw our doors open.

Inside the rarely used but hastily refurbished ballroom guests drank champagne and feasted on canapés and my father gave a painfully false speech. I only managed to sit through it by reaching into my pocket and clutching the envelope within.

The moment the speeches were done Axios was swarmed upon by fawning acquaintances, eager to engage the great man in conversation. I told myself that my primary emotion was relief as the stylists, also roped into acting as my attendants, rushed to straighten my veil and train, twitching and tweaking until they were satisfied that I'd been restored to their vision of bridal beauty.

But just when I thought I'd have a moment's reprieve Axios's gaze zeroed in on me, his eyes falling to the barely touched food on the plate that lay next to my untouched glass of champagne.

One brow rose. 'Not in the mood for celebrating? Or are you trying to make some sort of point by not eating?'

I couldn't eat—not when the inkling was deepening that Axios Xenakis was far from a willing participant in this devilish deal. And if that was the case, what had I let myself in for?

I pushed the anxious thought away and let my gaze fall on his equally full plate. 'You should talk.'

He lifted his champagne and took a healthy gulp. 'Unlike you, this occasion isn't one I feel inclined to celebrate.'

My breath caught, but before I could ask him to elaborate, he continued.

'And in the interest of clarity let me warn you

that neither you nor your father have any cards left to play. Should you feel inclined to make *more* demands.'

Christos, what exactly had my father done?

But even as the question burned fire boiled in my blood. 'Are you threatening my family? Because if you are, please know that I will fight you with everything I've got.'

His lips twisted at my fierce tone. 'What a fiery temper you have. I wonder what other surprises you're hiding beneath those unfortunate layers of... What *is* that material?'

As much as I hated my wedding dress, his remark sparked irritation. 'It's called tulle. And you should know. You paid for it, after all.'

The barest hint of a sardonic smile lifted his sensual lips. 'Writing a cheque for it doesn't mean I pay attention to every single detail of a woman's wardrobe. I have better things to do than concern myself with the name of the fabric that comprises a wedding gown.'

'But this is *your* wedding too,' I taunted, knowing my mockery would aggravate.

Something about this towering hunk of a man, who'd made it clear that this was the last place he wanted to be, riled me on a visceral level, firing up a need to dig beneath his formidable exterior.

'Isn't it supposed to be one of the momentous occasions of your life?'

Every trace of humour disappeared. Piercing grey eyes pinned me in place, and the tension vibrating from him was so thick I could almost touch it.

'Momentous occasions are highly anticipated and satisfactorily celebrated. You'd have to be delusional or deliberately blind to imagine I'm in such a state, Calypso Petras.'

The way he said my name, with drawling, mocking intonation, fired my blood. Along with other sensations I couldn't quite name.

'It's Calypso Xenakis now—or have you already forgotten?' I fired back, taking secret pleasure in seeing the irritated flare of his nostrils.

'I have not forgotten,' he answered with taut iciness.

'If this is such an ordeal for you, then why all this?' I waved my hand at the obscenely lavish banquet displayed along one long wall, the champagne tower brimming with expensive golden bubbles, the caviar-laden trays being circulated, and the designer-clad guests, shamelessly indulging their appetites.

'Because your father insisted,' he replied, his voice colder than an arctic vortex. 'As *you* well know.'

I opened my mouth to tell him for once and for all that none of this made sense to me because no one had bothered to consult me about my own wedding.

The sight of my mother's face, staring at me from one table away, pain and misery etched beneath her smile, dried the words in my throat.

For whatever reason fate had tangled the Xenakises and the Petrases in an acrimonious weave and my mother and I were caught in the middle. I could no more extricate myself than I could turn my back on her.

A tiny, tortured sound whistled through the air and I realised it came from my own throat—a manifestation of that hysteria that just wouldn't die down. I stood abruptly, knowing I had to get away before I did something regrettable.

Like climb on top of the lavishly decorated lonely high table, set apart from everyone else to showcase the newly married couple in all their glory, and scream at the top of my lungs.

That just wouldn't do. Because while I might have acquired a new surname, it was dawning on me that until I learned the true nature of what I was embroiled in I would be wise to keep a firm hold of my feelings.

And an even firmer hold of my wits.

CHAPTER TWO

MONEY MAKES THE world spin.

I swallowed my champagne, careful not to choke on it as I dispassionately observed the guests indulging in the revelry of my sham of a wedding.

Money had made this happen, and in the exact time frame I'd requested it.

Money had put that smug smile on Yiannis Petras's face.

Money had made the family, decimated by my grandfather's fall from grace, rally together for the sake of enjoying the rejuvenated fruits of my labour.

I'd seen first-hand how the lack of it could cause backbiting and untold strain. Ostensibly solid marriages crumbled under the threat of diminished wealth and influence. I'd seen it in my parents' marriage. It was why I'd never have freely chosen this route for myself.

My gaze shifted to my brand-new wife.

Had money influenced her agreement to this fiasco?

Was she getting a cut of the hundred million euros?

Of course she was. Had she not proclaimed herself a true Petras?

For those seconds as she'd hesitated at the altar I'd entertained the notion that she shared my reluctance, had imagined the merest hint of resistance in her eyes.

Her words had put me straight.

A cursory investigation had revealed that while she'd graduated from Skypos University with a major in Arts, she'd done nothing with her degree for the last two years. Her father's daughter through and through, sitting back and taking the easy route to riches.

So what if outwardly she wasn't what I expected?

I snorted under my breath at this colossal understatement. Calypso Petras...*ochi*, make that Calypso Xenakis...was beyond a surprise. She was a punch to my solar plexus, one it was taking an irritatingly long time to wrestle under control.

Even now my senses still reeled from what I'd uncovered beneath her veil. She was far from the drab little mouse I'd assumed.

'I believe there's a rule somewhere that states you shouldn't scowl on your wedding day.'

I resisted the urge to grind my teeth and faced my brother. 'You think this is funny?'

'This whole circus? No. I believe that ring on your finger and the look on your face makes it all too real.' Neo affected a mocking shudder intended to rile me further.

It worked.

'I'm talking about your implication that my... Calypso.' *Thee mou*, why did her name sound so...erotic?

Neo's eyes widened before glinting with keen speculation. 'If I recall, I didn't give you any specifics.'

There was a reason Neo was president of marketing at Xenakis Aeronautics. He could sell hay to a farmer.

My fingers tightened around my glass. 'You deliberately let me to think she was...unremarkable.'

She was quite the opposite. Hers was the confounding kind of beauty one couldn't place a finger on. The kind that made you stare for much longer than was polite.

Neo shrugged. 'No, I didn't. And don't blame me for the dire state of your mind, brother,' he answered.

The low heat burning through my blood intensified. And while I wanted to attribute it to this conversation, I knew I couldn't. Ever since I'd pulled that hideous veil off her face and uncovered the woman I'd agreed to marry a different irritation had lodged itself deep inside me. One I wasn't quite ready to examine.

But that wasn't to say I was ready to let Neo off the hook for…

For what?

Making obfuscating observations about Calypso Petras that had made me dismiss her from my mind, only to be knocked off-kilter by her appearance?

Granted, she still wasn't my type. Her eyes were too large…much too *distracting*. They were the type of turquoise-blue that made you question their authenticity. Framed with long eyelashes that begged the same question. And then there were her lips. Full and sensual, with a natural bruised rose hue, and deeply alluring despite the absence of gloss.

The dichotomy of fully made-up eyes and bare lips had absorbed my attention for much too long at that altar. And it had irritated me even further that since our arrival at the reception those lips had been buried beneath a hideous layer of frosty peach.

But it hadn't stopped me puzzling over why the two aspects of her initial appearance had been so

at odds with each other. Or why she'd seemed…
startled by our very brief kiss on the altar.

False innocence wrapped around her true character? A character that contained more than a
little fire.

My mind flicked to other hints I'd glimpsed
over the last few hours. While I was yet to discover what lay beneath the layers of the wedding
gown, there were more than enough hints to au-
thenticate her voluptuousness.

Yet to discover…

The peculiar buzz that had been ignited during that fleeting kiss notched up a fraction, the
fact that the brief contact still lingered on my
lips drawing another frown.

'Your new wife is looking a little…unhappy.
Perhaps you should see about fixing that?'

About to state that I had nothing to fix, that her
happiness was none of my concern, I found my
gaze flicked to the table. Despite the picture of
poise she was trying to project she looked pale,
her eyes flitting nervously. A quick scrutiny of
our guests showed she was the object of several
stares and blatant whispers.

A helpless prey in a jungle of predators.

My feet moved almost of their own accord,
the niggling urge to reverse that look on her face

irritating me even as I moved towards her, effectively silencing the whispers with quelling stares.

Regardless of how this union had come about, rumours couldn't be allowed to run rife. This was how undermining started.

As I neared, silence fell. Her gaze shifted, met mine. Her chin lifted, a wisp of bewilderment and skittishness evaporating and her eyes flashing with defiance.

For some absurd reason it sparked something to life inside me. Something I fully intended to ignore.

Defiance or bewilderment, the deed was done. She and her family had capitalised on an agreement made under duress and bagged themselves a windfall. She should be celebrating.

Instead I caught another trace of apprehension as I stopped beside her chair. Eyes growing wide, she looked up at me. The graceful line of her neck—another alluring feature that seemed to demand attention—rippled as she swallowed.

Thee mou, if this was an act then she was a good actress!

Aware of our audience, and a burning need to find out, I held out my hand to her. 'The traditional first dance is coming up, I believe.' The earlier we could get this spectacle out of the way, the quicker I could resume my life.

Her gaze darted to the dance floor, her reluctance clear. 'Is that…really necessary?'

Something about her reluctance and her whole demeanour grated. She was behaving as if I was contaminated!

'Enough with this pretence. That wide-eyed innocent thing will only work for so long. Give it up, Calypso.'

She offered me her hand, but the eyes that met mine as she stood sparkled with renewed fire. 'No one calls me Calypso. My name is Callie,' she stated firmly.

I attempted to ignore the slim fingers in mine, the smooth softness of her palm and the way it kicked to life something inside me as I led her to the middle of the dance floor.

'I'm your new husband—surely I don't fall under the category of *no one*?' I curled my arm around her waist, a singular need to press her close escalating inside me as the band struck up a waltz.

She stiffened. 'Are you insinuating that you're *special*?'

For some reason my lips quirked. 'By your tone, I'm guessing I'm not. Not even special enough for you to grant me the simple gift of addressing you as I please?'

Her lips firmed again, drawing my attention

to their plumpness. Reminding me of that all too fleeting taste of them.

'And what am I to call *you*? Other than *stranger* or *husband*?'

For some reason the fiery huskiness of her voice drew another smile. A puzzle in itself, since humour was the last emotion I should have been experiencing. I was in this situation because of money and shameless greed.

'Call me Axios. Or Ax, as most people do. I doubt we will reach the stage of coining terms of endearment.'

'On that I think we're agreed,' she replied, her gaze fixed somewhere over my shoulder.

Another scrabble of irritation threatened to rise, but I suppressed it when I noticed that once again, beneath the show of sharp claws, she was trembling, her wide eyes a little too bright. As if she was holding on to her composure by a thread.

'Is something wrong?' I asked. Again I questioned my need to know. Or care.

'What could possibly be wrong?'

She didn't bother to meet my gaze. If anything, she attempted to detach herself, which ought to have been impossible, considering how close we were dancing. But I was learning that my new wife had several…interesting facets.

'It is polite to look at me when you address me.'

She maintained her stance for another few seconds, then her blue eyes rose to mine. The urge to stare into them, to commit every fleck and expression to memory, charged through me, this time bringing a wave of heat to my groin.

I inhaled slowly, forcing myself to ignore that unsettling sensation and address her as I would any acquaintance.

Even though she wasn't.

Even though she'd taken my name and we were effectively bound together for twelve long months.

'This thing will go smoother if we attempt to be civil with one another. Don't you agree?'

'I'm not a puppet. I cannot act a certain way on command.'

'But you *can* dispense with that little-girl-lost look. And I find it curious that you would choose to refer to puppets. Perhaps you're familiar with knowing exactly which strings to tug to get what you want?'

Unlike me, she didn't attempt to disguise her frown. 'What are you talking about?'

'This whole scheme, orchestrated by you and your family, has gone off without a hitch. Feel free to stop acting now.'

She inhaled sharply, her eyes darting to the

guests dancing around us. 'Please keep your voice down.'

'Afraid you'll be found out? Are you really so blind to the fact that every single guest is speculating wildly about how two people who've never met are now married?'

Her plump lips pressed together for a moment. 'I can't control what other people think. But I do care about perpetuating unfounded rumours.'

'Do you, *yineka mou*?'

Her blue eyes shadowed and her gaze quickly flicked away. 'Can you not call me that, please?'

'Why not? Are you not my wife?'

The more the term fell from my lips the deeper it bored into me, as if rooting for a place to settle. Of course the search would be futile, because this was far from what I wanted.

The strain and stress of trying to save his failing company while keeping his family and his marriage together had driven my grandfather into an early grave, his spirit broken long before the heart attack that had suddenly taken him. It was the same stress that had nearly broken my own father, forcing him to step down after a mere two years as CEO.

I didn't intend to weigh myself down with similar baggage.

I refocused on Calypso, attempting to ignore

the effect of her soft curves against my body as she asked, 'So, what happens after this?'

'"This"?'

'After we're done here,' she elaborated.

Unbidden, my thoughts flew ahead. To when the evening would turn exclusive and intimate. When wedding euphoria traditionally took on another, more carnal dimension.

A traditions I *wouldn't* be indulging in.

'Do you plan on getting back into your helicopter and leaving me here?'

The carefully disguised hope in her voice threw me back to that day in my father's office a month ago, when an agreement that bore all the hallmarks of blackmail had crash-landed into my life and threatened the Xenakis name and business. Did she really think she and her family could take financial advantage and then sail off into the sunset?

The silent vow I'd taken that day to ensure neither Calypso nor her father escaped unscathed resurged as I looked down into her face. A face struggling for composure and a body twitching nervously beneath my hand.

I pulled her closer, steadied her at her slight stumble, and lowered my lips to her ear.

'It's our wedding night, *matia mou*. How would

it look if we didn't stay under the same roof? Sleep in the same bed?'

My lips brushed the delicate shell of her ear and she shivered. A moment later wide, alluring eyes sought mine.

'Sleep in the same bed? But you don't even know me. What...what's the rush?'

I opened my mouth to tell her there was no rush. That giving her my name was the final payment she and her family would extract from me. Instead I shrugged, noting absently that a part of me was enjoying this a little too much.

'Other than ensuring there will be nothing to be held over my head when the whim takes your father? Are you suggesting a period of getting to know one another before we decide if we must consummate this marriage?'

She gave a little start. '*If?* Don't you mean *when*?' she whispered fiercely, her eyes wider, searching.

Again the words to answer, to state that this dance was as close as we would get for the duration of our agreement, remained unsaid on the tip of my tongue. If she believed I would further compound this debacle by gracing her bed, so be it. She would discover differently later.

Absurdly, the pleasure in that thought of delivering disappointment never arrived. Instead

I was unarmed by a disturbing throbbing in my groin, by the temptation to take a different approach. To gather her closer, breathe in the alluring perfume that clung to her silken skin.

I did just that, nudging her close with a firm clasp on her lower back. And heard her sharp intake of breath.

Pulling back, I glanced at her pale face. 'Are you all right?'

Her swift nod assured me that she was lying, and the wild darting of her gaze confirmed that belief.

'Calypso?'

'I… I'm fine. Just a little headache. That's all.'

I frowned. 'Then why are you touching your stomach?'

Her hand quickly relocated from her midriff to my shoulder, her smile little more than a grimace. 'It's nothing, I assure you.'

About to refute that assurance, I was forestalled by the end of the music and the applause that followed. And then by the arrival of Iona Petras.

My introduction to Calypso's mother, along with everyone else in the Petras clan, had been stiff and perfunctory, with no disguising exactly what this bloodless transaction was.

Everyone except Calypso.

'May I have a private moment with my daughter?' the older woman asked, although I got the feeling it was more an order than a request, giving me a momentary glimpse of where Calypso had inherited her quiet fire.

My fingers started to tighten on Calypso's waist, as a peculiar reluctance to let her go assailed me. I strenuously denied it and released her. 'By all means.'

A silent conversation passed between mother and daughter before Calypso held out her hand. Without so much as a glance my way, they exited the ballroom.

A fine irritant, like a tiny pebble in my shoe, stayed with me throughout all my inane conversations with people I didn't know and another five-minute ribbing from Neo. By the time my father approached I had the notion that my jaw would crack from being ground so tight.

'Am I mistaken or do you two seem to be getting along?' my father asked.

'You are mistaken,' I quipped, unwilling to admit how that dance and the feel of Calypso in my arms had fired up my blood.

He grimaced. 'I was hoping this would be less of an ordeal for you if you got along.'

'I said I'd do what needs to be done. And I will.'

Despite that small, startling flame of anticipation burning inside me.

Despite the fact that I'd completely dismissed any occurrence of a wedding night until exactly five minutes ago.

That sensation of her slender back beneath my hand…that pulse beating at her throat… The shivers she couldn't control.

The fire of anticipation flared higher, resisting every attempt to dampen it down.

But did I need to?

This abhorrent agreement hadn't, thankfully, included a stipulation for consummation. But would it be a true marriage without it?

Enough!

Wrestling with myself over this was beneath me. Everything Yiannis Petras had asked for had been delivered. They would get nothing more from me.

That declaration lasted until my new wife walked back into the room and attempted to dismiss me with a vacant smile, even while her eyes challenged me.

Something locked into place inside me.

A challenge that needed answering.

Without stopping to question the wisdom of doing it, I crossed the wide room to where she stood. Took the hand loosely fisted by her side and brushed my lips over her knuckles.

Satisfaction sizzled through me when her breath caught. 'Say your goodbyes, Calypso. It's time to leave.'

'So what now?' I cringed inwardly at the nerves in my voice.

The helicopter ride—my first—from Nicrete to Agistros, the large island apparently owned entirely by Axios, had been breathtaking and exhilarating, and thankfully had not required much conversation. Largely because Axios had piloted the aircraft and I'd felt too nervous to disturb him, even if there'd been anything to talk about.

My mind was still a jumble after our charged snippets of conversation and that little slip on the dance floor, when he pulled me close and the ache in my belly manifested itself, and my last unsettling conversation with my mother.

But most of all it was the look in Axios's eyes before he'd whisked me away from the reception and down to the waiting helicopter that kept my heart banging against my ribs.

That look was far too unsettling and electrifying for me to rest easy.

Especially not after landing on a dedicated cliff-side helipad on this island that boasted its own dormant volcano and a jaw-dropping villa that seemed almost too beautiful to be real.

I thought it was the setting sun that leant it that fairy tale look and made the unevenly staggered storeys seem to go on for ever. But every single facet of it turned out to be real, from the blush-hued stone, the towering arched windows, the rooftop infinity pool that seemed to blend into the sky and the endless reception rooms and bedroom suites, each holding priceless ancient works of art interspersed with the work of new cutting-edge artists whose work I loved.

Every jaw-dropping fact I'd read about Axios Xenakis had seemed amplified the moment he'd stepped out of the helicopter, and his aura was intensifying with each second as he walked me around Villa Almyra, exuding flawless power and authority.

Now, standing in the luxury sitting room adjoining what I assumed to be the master bedroom, I couldn't hold my words back.

He didn't answer for the longest time. He shrugged off the bespoke jacket he'd worn for the wedding ceremony. Then strolled over to the extensive drinks cabinet.

'Would you like a drink?' he asked.

About to refuse, I stopped. It would buy me time to ease my nerves. 'Mineral water, thanks.'

He poured my drink, then a single malt whisky into a crystal glass, handing mine to me before taking his time to savour his first sip.

The feeling that he was waiting, biding his time for...*something* threatened to overwhelm me, even while my senses skittered with alien excitement. Slowly it grew hotter, more dangerous.

His gaze raked over my wedding dress for a charged few seconds. 'Now we do whatever you want. It's *your* wedding night after all,' he drawled.

I got the feeling he was testing me. For what, I didn't know. And I wasn't sure I was ready to find out.

'The modern art pieces all over the house. Did you pick them yourself?'

His eyes widened fractionally, as if I'd surprised him. 'Yes,' he bit out. Then, on a softer note, 'Good art rarely loses its value.'

A layer of my nerves eased as I nodded. 'And pieces from emerging talent only appreciate with time.'

He strolled to the massive fireplace in the living room and leaned one muscular shoulder against the mantel. 'Masterpieces from the greats are all well and good, but modern art has its place too. They should be appreciated side by side.'

Just as he had placed them all over the house. I took a sip of water, settling deeper into my seat. 'I agree. Does that theme echo in all your properties?'

'Yes, it does.'

Before I could express pleasure in the thought, the gleam in his eyes arrested me.

'Is this how you wish to spend your wedding night, Calypso? Discussing art?'

The nerves rushed back and my hand trembled. 'What if it is?'

'Then I suggest you might want to be in more comfortable attire than that gown?'

Again, his eyes raked me, sending heat spiralling through me.

'Is this a ploy that usually works for you?'

One corner of his mouth lifted before his eyes darkened. 'Like you, I've never been married, so we both find ourselves in strange waters. Either way, the dress is going to have to come off one way or the other.'

'And if you don't like what is underneath…?' I dared. 'Will you send me back?'

His eyes narrowed. 'Is that what you're hoping for?'

Was it? I could have sworn my answer would be yes until actually faced with the question. But the word stuck in my throat, refusing to emerge as he sauntered towards me, taking a moment to discard the crystal tumbler so both his hands were free to capture my shoulders when he stopped in front of me.

'What I'm hoping for is that you will stop dishing out those enigmatic smiles and tell me what you meant earlier,' I said.

He frowned. 'You've lost me,' he drawled.

'When you said *if* we were to consummate this marriage? Are you incapable of doing so? If so perhaps you should get one of your staff to show me where I'm to sleep.'

His eyebrows rose. 'If I didn't know better I'd think you just issued me a challenge,' he drawled, in a voice that ruffled the tight nerves beneath my skin.

His scent filled my nostrils, his calm breathing propelling my attention to his sculpted chest, to the pulse beating steadily at his throat. To the magnificent vitality of his skin and the sheer animalistic aura breaching my tightly controlled space. Screaming at me to notice his masculinity. And not just to notice. He drew me with a power I'd never known before. I didn't just want to breathe him in. I wanted to touch. Explore. Taste.

That sensation was so strong I stepped back, eager to diffuse it.

The hands that held me stemmed my movement, and hard on the heels of my immobility
came the realisation that I wanted to stay right
where I was. But I didn't want him to know that.

'Well? *Are* you?' I taunted.

A mysterious smile tilted one corner of his
lips before his hands slid down to my elbows.
'It should be easy enough to prove, *matia mou.*'

Just like that I was hit with the reality that this
was my wedding night. That I was all but taunting him into...*possessing* me.

The thought sent a shiver through me. Coupled
with something else. Something way too close
to the forbidden desire that had coursed through
me when I'd allowed myself to dream of this day
some time in the dim and distant future, when I
was out from under my father's thumb and free
to have a boyfriend. A lover. A *husband.*

But how could that be? The man I'd imagined
bore no resemblance to this formidable man,
who wore arrogance and power as if it were a
second skin. *Theos*, even his frown was atten-
tion-absorbing.

'Are you cold?' he asked.

I shook my head. Like everything else in this
stunning villa, the temperature was perfect,
blending with the early summer breeze.

'Then what's wrong?' he rasped, his eyes turning speculative again, as they had when I almost gave myself away on the dance floor.

The pain had thankfully receded, but other questions loomed just as large. The subject of my virginity and how that would factor into things, for one.

I pushed it away, seizing on another pressing need. 'I want you to tell me exactly what your agreement with my father is.'

One eyebrow rose. 'Isn't that a case of shutting the barn door after the horse has bolted? What's the point of rehashing the subject?'

It was time to come clean. 'I… I may have let you operate under the assumption that I know what's going on.'

Surprise flickered through his eyes before they narrowed. 'Are you saying you don't?'

'Not the exact details, no.'

Scepticism flared. 'You expect me to believe that? When you walked willingly by his side up the aisle?'

'Tell me you've never done something against your will and I'll call you a liar,' I replied.

The flare of his nostrils confirmed what I suspected—that this marriage was as much without his approval as it was without mine.

'Assuming it was solely your father who pushed for this, what steps did you take to stop him?'

None. Because my protests, like everything else, had fallen on deaf ears. I didn't say the words out loud, his timely reminder that, despite the promise I'd made, my mother's fate was in my father's hands, stilling my tongue. My hesitation gave Axios the answer he needed.

'I didn't, and the details don't matter. We are where we are. But I know there's an agreement between you. I simply want you to spell it out for me so I know what I'm dealing with.'

He stared at me, his measuring gaze weighted. I shouldn't have been relieved, even a little pleased to see the cynicism fade a little, but I was.

'Maybe he didn't tell you. How very like Petras to want to keep the spoils all for himself,' he muttered almost absently, before dropping his hands from my arms to say abruptly, 'Under an agreement signed between your grandfather and mine, Yiannis Petras, or any appointed representative after his death, can collect on a debt owed by my family. Your father wanted twenty-five percent of my company or the cash equivalent. We settled on one hundred million euros. And you.'

I couldn't hide my gasp at the confirmation that I'd been sold like a chattel.

Again, his cynicism receded. 'He really didn't

tell you? Are you saying you're a victim in this?' he breathed.

The label smarted. 'I'm not a victim. But, no, he didn't tell me.'

Jaw gritted, he shoved a hand through his hair. 'So you don't know that under the terms of the agreement he'll also receive the deeds to Kosima?'

'What is Kosima?'

A bleak expression darkened his face. Whatever Kosima was, it held an emotional attachment for him.

'It's the private island where my grandfather was born. It was his favourite place on earth. Your grandfather knew that when he and my grandfather struck their unholy agreement. I assume he passed the information on to your father.'

My heart lurched with guilt, and for a wild moment I wanted to ease his pain. 'And my father demanded it as part of the agreement?'

Again his lips twisted, before his gaze slanted over me from head to toe. 'Of course. Just as he demanded that I marry *you*.'

This time my heart lurched for a different reason. He truly hadn't wanted this marriage—was entangled in it against his will just as I was.

About to stress that I had known absolutely

nothing about this, that my father's avaricious demands were nothing to do with me, I heard that stern warning from my father slam into my brain. I didn't doubt that he would make my mother's life even more of a living hell than it was now.

The realisation that nothing had changed, that nothing *would* change, settled on me like a heavy, claustrophobic cloak.

'Why did you go through with it?' I asked. When he frowned, I hurried to add, 'You obviously hate what my family has done to you, so why…?'

My disjointed thoughts rumbled to a halt, my insides twisting with dread. A caged lion was an unpredictable creature, and from the first moment I'd set eyes on him I'd felt his banked fury.

Now I knew why.

His eyes blazed grey fire at me. 'You think I didn't try to find a way that didn't involve tying myself down for twelve months or handing over a multi-million-euro pay-out your father has done *nothing* to earn?' he sliced at me.

My breath caught. 'Why twelve months? Why not three…or even six?'

His mouth tightened. 'Ask your father. He had the power to nullify some or all aspects of this agreement. He chose not to. And he counted on me not fighting this in court because adverse publicity is the last thing my company needs right now. Your grandfather was an unreasonable man who my own grandfather had the misfortune of partnering with.'

'I know they started the airline business together, but—'

'Your grandfather wasn't interested in an airline business. He wanted to invest in boats, despite knowing next to nothing about them,' he spat out the words. 'But because they were tied together my grandfather was forced to work twice as hard to maintain both arms of the business. The only way Petras would agree to dissolve the partnership was to leave without taking his quarter-of-a-million-dollar share of the business immediately. If he had done so he would've bankrupted the company. But that didn't stop him from demanding crippling interest on the loan, and an agreement promising a percentage of Xenakis Aeronautics should he or any other Petras need a future bail-out. But even then, it was too late. My grandfather had spread himself too thin, trying to maintain two suffering businesses, but he was too proud to declare bankruptcy. The strain broke his marriage and his family, and after my grandmother died his heart just…gave up.'

My heart twisted at the anguish in his voice. 'I…'

What could I say? *I'm sorry*? Would Axios even believe me? What did it matter? My father had cunningly used the past against him. Against both of us.

'I didn't know any of this.'

His jaw rippled. 'My grandfather was my mentor. He taught me everything I know. But he withheld the extent of how bad things were until it was too late. Until I had to watch him wither away.'

After an age of losing himself in the bleak past, his eyes zeroed in on me.

'Why? If you didn't know all this, why present yourself to me at that altar like a sacrificial lamb?'

The cynicism was back full force. 'I'm not a lamb!'

One corner of his mouth lifted. 'No, I'm learning that my initial impression was mistaken. But I still want to know why,' he pressed with quiet force.

How could I tell him without speaking of the very thing I'd done all this to avoid? If my father had managed to pressure a powerful man like Axios Xenakis to do his will, what would he do to my mother if he found out I'd been divulging family secrets?

'Perhaps I had something to gain too,' I responded truthfully, knowing how it would be viewed.

True to form, his eyes slowly hardened, and that disappointment I'd briefly spotted at the altar flashed across his face.

As one of his hands slowly rose to cup my face, it seemed he wanted to delve deeper, perhaps even attempt to understand how we had become caught in this tangled web. But then he slowly withdrew, his demeanour resigned, even a little weary.

An urge to soothe him spiked through me. I managed to curb it, barely managing not to fidget under his piercing scrutiny.

'Did the agreement stipulate that we needed to...to consummate the marriage?' I asked.

He froze, and a sizzling, electrifying look entered his eyes. I got the feeling that he'd been waiting for this...that somehow coming to this point was what that sense of heightened expectancy had been all about.

'Not specifically, no.'

'But you don't know that it won't be held against you…against us…further down the line?'

He gave an indolent shrug even while his eyes continued to pin me in place. 'He's *your* father, Calypso. You tell me.'

I couldn't rule it out. And I suspected Axios knew that.

'Maybe he will. Maybe he won't. But I can't take the risk.'

With my mother's words echoing in my heart, my hunger for freedom grew with every second.

He took a slow, steady step towards me. His hands at his sides, he simply stared down at me, his only movement the deep rise and fall of his chest.

'What does that mean, Calypso?' he queried softly.

'It means I want there to be no room for misunderstanding later.'

Slowly, his hand rose again, his knuckles grazing my cheek. My shiver made his eyes darken.

'I need to hear the words, so there's no misunderstanding now.'

Heat suffused my face, as if chasing his touch. But his gaze wouldn't release me. Not until the words trembling on my lips fell free.

'I want to consummate this agreement. I want you to…take me.'

The full force of the words powered through me, shaking me from head to foot. Dear God, this wasn't how I'd imagined losing my virginity. None of this was how I'd dreamed it. So why did my insides twist themselves with...*excitement*?

For the longest time he simply stared at me, a myriad of emotions crossing his face. Eventually that dark gleam returned in full force, his presence filling the room as he turned his hand and brushed a thumb over my lips.

'Are you sure you don't wish to discuss...art?'

The thickness of his voice displaced any levity his words attempted. And it drove home that this was happening. My wedding night. No, it wasn't the one I'd dreamed about, but really, if life was fair, would my father have tossed me in as part of a hundred-million-euro deal?

That thought was buried beneath the turbulent need climbing through me as he dragged his digit back and forth over my lip.

'I'm sure,' I answered, in a voice that sounded nothing like mine.

He tilted my gaze to his, making a gruff sound at whatever it was he saw on my face. His head started to lower—just as the other delicate subject raced to the forefront of my mind.

Tell him. He's going to find out soon enough.

'There's something you should know.'

One eyebrow rose in silent question.

'I'm a virgin.'

His fingers froze beneath my chin, his whole body turning to marble. 'What did you say?'

I swallowed the knot in my throat, praying the shivers would stop coursing through my body. 'I've never done…never been with a—'

A curse fell from his lips, raw and stunned. 'Why?'

Finally—*finally*—that burst of hysteria filtered through. 'You're asking why your wife is a virgin? Isn't that an odd question?'

'*Ne*—and it is precisely why I want to know why a twenty-four-year-old who looks the way you do is still untouched.'

Heat flowed through me. 'Looks the way I do…?'

The faintest colour washed his cheekbones. 'You must be aware of your beauty, Calypso,' he rasped, and his deep, husky voice set fire to my belly.

I blushed at the raw intensity in his words that reached into a secret part of me and took control of it. Hot tingles raced over my skin, warming me from the inside, tightening low in my belly and hardening my nipples. A gasp tore from my throat. His gaze dropped to my parted lips, his eyes darkening with each charged second that ticked by.

Then his eyes narrowed. 'Surely Petras didn't keep you under lock and key simply for this possibility?' Incredulity racked his voice.

Pain lashed through me, because the same thought had occurred to me. My father might not have visited the ultimate indignity upon me by spelling it out in black and white, but by thwarting all my previous attempts at a relationship he'd ensured his deal would be sweetened with my virginity. Another indication as to how little he cared for me.

Despite the anguish racking me, I raised my chin, pride insisting I did not confirm his suspicion. 'Does it not occur to you that I've simply not met anyone interesting enough?'

Shrewd grey eyes conducted a slow scrutiny. 'Your pulse is racing. Your face is flushed. I don't need a crystal ball to tell me you're excited. It is safe to say that, regardless of why you've remained untouched before, you're definitely interested now, Calypso.'

I silently cursed my body for betraying me but I wasn't ready to be cowed yet. 'You want me to bolster your ego by admitting I find you attractive?'

His head went back, as if he was surprised

by the question. Of course he did. Good looks. Power. Influence. All attributes that made him irresistible to women. The stunning parade of women he'd purportedly dated was evidence that his effect on the opposite sex was woven into his DNA.

A sexy, arrogant smile curved his lips. 'I don't need you to *tell* me, *matia mou*. I *know* you do.'

My gasp was swallowed by the simple act of his head swooping down and his mouth sealing mine in a hot, savage possession that snatched the breath from my lungs. If that kiss in the church had been spine-tingling, this complete mastery was nothing short of earth-shattering.

The bold sweep of his tongue over my sensitive lower lip fired electricity in every cell. When he followed that with the lightest graze of his teeth, in another clever tasting, a tiny hunger-filled sound left my throat.

Axios muttered something beneath his breath before the fingers capturing my chin moved to my lower back, tugging me closer, until the hard column of his body was plastered against mine and the wide stance of his powerful legs cradled me. Until the hot brand of his manhood was unmistakably imprinted against my belly, in a searing promise of what was in store.

His lips devoured mine with unapologetic hunger. And when one hand grasped mine and redirected it to his chest I gave in to the heady desire and explored him. Tensile muscle overlaid by his expensive cotton shirt was warm and inviting, and after a tentative caress, I sighed and gave in to *more*. The ultra-masculine line of his shoulder and neck drew my fingers, and that mysterious hunger built up into something that both terrified and thrilled me.

He made a gruff sound when my fingers brushed his warm, supple throat. It was enough to startle me. Enough to remind me that I didn't really know what I was doing. That, while I understood the mechanics of sex, I wasn't well-versed in its nuances.

Nerves dulled by the fire of arousal resurged, breaking free by way of a helpless whimper.

He raised his head and stared at me for the longest time before catching my hand in his. 'Come,' he commanded huskily.

I snatched in a much-needed breath. We both knew where we stood—that we were products of my father's machinations—surely we were going into this with our eyes open, in the knowledge that this was a one-time thing…weren't we?

Molten grey eyes watched me. When I slid my hand into his, he led me to some wide, imposing double doors. With casual strength he pushed them open to reveal the most magnificent bedroom I'd ever seen. While it bore unashamed signs of masculinity, the Mediterranean blue hues of the furniture blended with solid wood and gold-trimmed furnishings in the kind of design afforded only to the rich and influential.

But of course the centrepiece of the huge space was the bed. Emperor-sized, with four solid posts, its only softening effect was the muslin curtains currently tied back with neat ribbons.

Axios released me long enough to toss away extraneous pillows and pull back the luxury spread before he recaptured me. This time both hands went to my waist, his gaze dropping down to where he held me. He muttered something under his breath that I couldn't quite catch and when our gazes reconnected flames danced in the dark grey depths.

My knees weakened and I lifted my hands to rest them on his shoulders. He drew me closer while his hands searched along my spine, located the zip to my dress and firmly drew it down.

The dress gaped and he drew in a harsh breath, his gaze trailing over my exposed skin to linger on my barely covered breasts. Through the silk his hands branded my skin, making me squirm with a need to feel them without any barrier. As if he heard my silent wish, he took hold of the straps and eased them down my arms. The material pooled at my feet, leaving me in the scrap of lace panties and matching strapless bra.

One expert flick and the bra was loosened. Instinctively, I moved to catch it. Moved to delay this exquisite madness unfurling inside me.

Axios caught my hand, drew it firmly back to his shoulder. 'I want to see you, Calypso. I want to see everything.'

Unable to stand the raw fire in his eyes, I fixed my eyes on his chest. On the buttons hiding that steel and muscle from me. Again he read my wants with ease.

'Take my shirt off, *yineka mou.*'

Yineka mou. My wife.

Why did my insides dance giddily each time he called me that? Especially when we both knew this was an enforced, transient thing?

'Don't keep me waiting.'

The husky nudge brought me back to him. With fingers that had given up being anywhere near steady, I reached for his sleekly knotted tie, tugged it free and released his top shirt button. It was simpler to avoid his eyes as I concentrated on my task, but halfway down, when my fingers brushed his abs, he hissed under his breath.

Impatience etched on his face, he took hold of the expensive cotton and pulled the shirt apart.

That raw display of strength tossed another log onto the flames building inside me. By the time he lifted me free of my wedding gown and took the few steps to the bed I'd lost the ability to breathe.

Riveted, I watched him shrug off the shirt, followed by his other clothing, before prowling to the bed. With the ease of a maestro he caught me to him, his fingers sliding up my nape and into my hair to release the three pins that secured the thick strands. His eyes raked my body as he slowly trailed his fingers through my hair. The effect was hot and hypnotising, the need to melt into him surging high.

So when he settled his expert lips over mine all I could do was moan and hold on, shudder in shocking delight when his chest grazed my hardened nipples.

But soon even that grew insufficient. Tentatively I parted my lips, in anticipation of the next decadent sweep of his tongue. When it grazed mine the zap of electricity convulsed my whole body.

Axios tore his lips from mine, incredulous eyes burning into me. 'You truly *are* innocent...' he muttered.

Mercifully, he didn't require an answer, or he was too impatient. After another searing kiss, in which his tongue breached my lips and brazenly slicked over mine, he trailed his lips over my throat.

Each pathway he claimed over my skin sent a pulse straight between my legs, plumping and heating my core until I thought I would explode. Large hands moulded my breasts, his fingers torturing the peaks. I cried out, my senses threatening to splinter.

The feeling of delving into another dimension, one where only pure pleasure existed, swelled through me, drawing me into a place of wonder. A place where I could give expression to what I was experiencing.

'That's...so amazing. How is this feeling possible?'

Had I said that out loud? Axios momentarily froze, but I was too caught up in bliss to find out why. Then his caresses continued, his mouth pressing kisses on my midriff, my belly, along the line of my panties.

When he tugged them down, my breath stalled.

He parted my thighs, trailed kisses up one inner thigh, then another.

'Your stubble feels...incredible.'

Again I felt him still.

'Am I doing something wrong? Please...'

Long fingers grazed the swollen nub, sending feverish pleasure racing through my body. Without him close to anchor me I grabbed hold of the sheets. Anything to keep me from disintegrating beneath the force of pleasure ramping through me.

Except that force tripled when his mouth settled with fierce intent on my feminine core. Brazenly, he tasted me with a connoisseur's expertise, teasing and torturing and dragging me to the brink of madness.

Until a new tightness took hold of me.

'Ah...it's too much... I... I can't take it...'

'Yes, you can,' he declared huskily.

His lips went back to wreaking their magic, to piling on that enchantment, until I simply... blew apart.

Bliss such as I'd never known suffused my body, convulsions rippling over me before sucking me under. I was aware of the cries falling from my lips, was aware that Axios had returned to my side, and I gripped him blindly, needing something solid to hang on to.

When he moved away I started to protest before I could stop myself. His kiss settled me for the few moments while he left the bed. The sound of foil ripping barely impinged upon my enchanted calm, my senses only sparking to life when he resumed his overwhelming presence between my thighs.

The intensity of the eyes locked on mine was almost too much to bear. I sought relief elsewhere. But there was none to be found in the wide expanse of his shoulders, the ripped contours of the chest I suddenly yearned to explore with my mouth, or… *Theos mou*…the fearsomely impressive evidence of his maleness.

The tiniest whimper slipped free. And while it brought an arrogant little twitch to his lips, there was also a slight softening of his fierce regard.

'Look at me, Calypso.'

The low command brought my gaze back to his. To the lock of hair grazing his eyebrow that I yearned to brush back. The slightly swollen sensual lips I wanted to kiss.

'Do you want this?' he asked.

The thought of stopping now was unthinkable. 'Yes,' I answered.

He gripped one thigh, parting me with unwavering intent.

The first shallow thrust stilled my breath. The second threw me back to that dimension where only sensation reigned.

Apprehensively, I exhaled. Axios moved his powerful body, withdrawing before penetrating me. Once. Twice.

On the third glide the sting was replaced by a different, jaw-dropping sensation, one that dragged me deeper into that dimension.

'You're…so deep. It feels…incredible.'

Above me, Axios hissed, his fingers digging into my thigh as he held himself, still and throbbing, inside me. The sensation was indescribable. But…

'Why aren't you moving? Do *I* need to? Maybe if I roll my hips…'

Tentatively I experimented, then cried out as pleasure rained over me.

'That was…sensational. I want to… Would you mind if I did it again?'

'No. I wouldn't,' he said thickly, then met my next thrust with an even more powerful one.

What the hell was happening?

I stared down at Calypso. Her eyes were shut in unbound pleasure.

My fraying control took another hit, the feeling that this little witch with her wide streak of innocence that had turned out not to be a clever trick was responsible for my curious state driving confusion through me.

The giving and taking of carnal pleasure was far from new to me but this…

I wanted to tell her to open her eyes. To centre her to me. To—

'Why are you stopping? Please don't stop. I want more.'

Her husky, innocent plea ramped up my arousal, the enormity of what was happening lending a savage edge to my hunger I'd never experienced before.

But just to be sure she was right there with me I leaned closer, flicked my tongue over her nipple. 'Do you like this, Calypso?'

Short blunt nails dug into my back. 'Yes!'

'And this?' I pulled the tight bud into my mouth, suckling her sweet flesh with fervour.

'*Ne*. That… You do that so well. I never want it to end.'

Theos. Did she not know what she was doing? That this kind of uncensored commentary could drive a man over the edge?

But she wasn't doing it with another man. She was doing it with *me*. The man she was bound to for the next twelve months.

Her husband.

Knowing I was her first shouldn't be sending such primitive satisfaction through my blood. And yet it was, settling deep inside me with such definitive force it threw up a shock of bewilderment.

I was thankful to avoid examining it in that moment. Because the utter nirvana of taking her, hearing her unfettered pleasure, was creating an unstoppable chain reaction inside me. One that kept me thrusting into her snug heat, my pulse racing to dangerous levels as her delicious lips parted and another torrent of words ran freely.

'*Glykó ouranó*... I'm on fire... What you're doing to me... Please... I need... I *need*...'

My teeth gritted as I hung on to control with my fingertips. As her sweet body arched beneath mine and her head thrashed on the pillow.

'You need to let go, Calypso.' I sounded barely coherent to my own ears.

With a sharp cry she gave herself over to her bliss, her sweet convulsions triggering mine. The depth of my climax left me gasping, the stars exploding across my vision unending.

Leached of all power and control, I collapsed onto the pillows, stunned by the sorcery I'd just experienced. A unique experience I wanted to relive again. Immediately.

Soft arms curved around my waist and I reached for her before I could stop myself— before I could question the wisdom of lingering when I normally exited. Pulling her into me when I normally distanced myself.

I will. In a moment.

Once I'd gathered myself. Once this experience had been dissected and slotted into its proper place.

I would have fought any future attempt by Yiannis Petras to further line his pocket, but Calypso's way of sealing all avenues had been… better. Pleasurable, even.

Or foolish?

I tensed, unwilling to accept that perhaps I could have found another way. Not succumbed to this bewitchment so readily.

So draw a line under it. Leave!

Her soft breathing feathered over my jaw. Sleep was stealing over her slightly flushed face. The urge to join her whispered over me—another wave of temptation that lingered for far too long, making me close my eyes for several minutes before common sense prevailed.

So what if the sex was sublime? It was just sex. Come tomorrow my life would resume its normal course. This whole day would be behind me.

I'd done my duty. Had ensured Petras would no longer be a threat to my family. For now the night was still young. There was no rush to go anywhere…

Except temptation was ten times stronger when I woke in the early hours of the morning. In the murky light of dawn I caught the faintest glimpse of the slippery slope my grandfather had been led down by another Petras.

A road I couldn't risk.

I put words to definitive action by rising and leaving the bed, gathering my clothes and walking out of the master bedroom.

Because my business with my wife was over.

CHAPTER THREE

MY TRANSITION FROM sleep to wakefulness was abrupt, bracing in the way that fundamental change manifested itself. Confirmation that I hadn't dreamt any of it registered in unknown muscles throbbing with new vigour. The sheets also bore evidence of what had happened, and confirmed that Axios had left some time in the night.

Had he chosen to sleep somewhere else? Or had his helicopter taken off during one of the brief stretches of time when I'd fallen asleep?

Although my agitated thoughts wanted to latch on to the fact that it was the sex that had driven him away, intuition suggested otherwise. Axios might not have wanted to experience the depth of chemistry that blazed between us but he'd been caught up too. Maybe a little bit too much?

Because I was reeling from the wildness of our coming together, the sheer abandonment that still rocked me to my core. The sheets might have cooled in his absence but his possession still remained. As did my growing consternation.

Last night my decision had seemed so clear-cut. Close all avenues by which my father could further interfere in my life. But the experience had been nothing like clear-cut. The experience of sleeping with Axios had been...unparalleled.

And now he was gone.

I refused to allow the dull thudding of my heart to dictate my disappointment. Whatever my future held, it was time for action.

About to get out of bed, I paused as my last conversation with my mother replayed one more time.

'You will know very quickly if this is the right choice for you. If it isn't, don't be like me. Don't accept it as inevitable. Do what is right for you.'

'What are you talking about, Mama?'

'Find your own happiness, Callie. Don't let your father's actions dictate the rest of your life. Your grandmother said the same thing to me on my wedding day and I didn't listen.'

'I don't think I have a choice. You... Papa—'

'Forget about me! There's nothing your father can do that will hurt me any more. Knowing you're unhappy because of me will break my heart. Promise me you'll put yourself first.'

'Mama—'

'Promise me, Callie!'

My promise weighed heavy on my heart as I rose from the bed. For a moment I swayed in place, my limbs weak with recollection and my body heating after every little wanton act of last night.

But, lips firmed, I approached what I hoped was the bathroom. There, further signs that this was Axios's domain were everywhere—from the luxury male products to the thick dark robe hanging next to the shower.

Trying not to let the intimacy of his belongings get to me, I quickly showered. Thankful for the voluminous towel that covered me from chest to ankle, I was contemplating the less than palatable thought of wearing my wedding dress again when a soft knock broke into my thoughts.

I cleared my throat. 'Come in.'

One of the younger staff members who helped manage the villa entered with a shy smile. She'd been introduced to me last night, when my senses had been grappling with unfolding events.

With a strained smile, I pulled the robe closer around me and returned her greeting.

Her gaze passed quickly over my towel. 'May I assist you with anything, *kyria*?'

'If you could direct me to where my belongings are, I'd appreciate it.'

'Of course. This way, please.'

Expecting her to leave the room, I was sur-

MAYA BLAKE

97

prised when she crossed to the opposite side and opened another door.

I followed her through a short hallway into another impressive suite, complete with living room, bathroom and dressing room.

An adjoining suite.

'I came to ask if you would like some breakfast, Kyria Xenakis?'

The title added another layer of shock to my system and it took me a few seconds to answer with a question of my own. 'Um…is Kyrios Xenakis still here?'

She nodded. 'Yes. But he will be leaving soon. So if you wish to—'

'Yes, I would very much like to. Can you wait for me to get dressed?'

Her eyes widened a touch, probably at the request. But I didn't care. I needed answers. Needed to know how he intended the next twelve months to proceed. And, if necessary, insist on taking back control of my life.

My father had shown me that he cared nothing about me except as a pawn to further his needs. Regardless of my commitment to Axios, I didn't intend to be pushed around any more.

That affirmation anchored deep as I concentrated on getting dressed.

The small suitcase that had accompanied me

when I left Nicrete was empty, its contents sitting on a lonely shelf in the vast dressing room. But those weren't the only contents of the large, opulent space. Rack upon rack of clothes were displayed in fashion seasons, with matching shoes arranged by colour, height and style.

Awestruck, I stared. It was by far the most extensive collection I'd seen outside a clothes store. Simply because I didn't know who the clothes in the closets belonged to, I fished out a simple shirt dress from my own belongings, added comfortable flats and caught my hair in a ponytail.

The maid led me down the stairs and through several halls before stopping at a set of double doors.

'He's in there,' she said softly. Then melted away.

The faint sound of clinking cutlery reached my ears as I paused to take a fortifying breath. But, aware that no amount of deep breathing could prepare me for the morning after last night, I pushed the door open.

He was seated at the head of a long, exquisitely laid table. Impeccably dressed in formal business attire, minus the jacket, with the sun streaming down on him.

I almost lost my footing at the sheer visceral impact of his masculinity. It really was unfair how attractive Axios Xenakis was. How the simple act of caressing his bottom lip with his forefinger, his brow furrowed in concentration, could spark fire low in my belly.

You're not here to ogle him.

Fists tightening at the reminder, I approached where he sat. 'We need to talk.'

He took his time to look up from the tablet propped up neatly next to his plate, to power it down with a flick of his finger before cool grey eyes tracked over me from head to toe and back again.

'*Kalimera*, Calypso. Sit down—have something to eat.'

His even tones threw me. He wasn't behaving like a man who'd left his marriage bed after bedding his virgin wife. In fact, he seemed far too confident. Far too...*together* for my liking.

When I didn't immediately obey he rose, his gaze resting on me as he pulled out a chair and... waited.

I sat, because hysteria would achieve nothing. What I intended to say to him could be said standing or sitting. Besides, this close, the potent mix of his warm body and his aftershave was making my head swim. Reminding me of what it had been like to stroke that warm body, to cling to it as fevered bliss overtook me.

'What's on your mind?' he enquired as he poured exquisite-smelling coffee into my cup, then nudged platters containing sliced meats, toast and cheeses towards me.

Cool. He was far too cool.

Something was going on here. I probed his face and saw the slight tension in his jaw. The banked emotion in his eyes. I might have known Axios for less than twenty-four hours, but I'd quickly deciphered that his eyes gave him away. Right now, they were far too shrewd.

My heart jumped into my throat.

'My father may have put us both in this position, but there's no reason why we should remain like this.' Relief welled as my voice emerged strong and steady.

His nod of agreement stunned me. 'You're right,' he said.

'I am?'

He shrugged. 'The agreement states that we should be married for a year minimum—not that we need to be in each other's pocket. Of course that's not to say it's cart blanche for you to do as you please.'

'What does *that* mean?'

'It means that for the time being Agistros is yours to enjoy. We will revisit our circumstances again when I return in a few weeks.'

His announcement was still resonating inside me when he rose from the table and strode, his head proud, shoulders stiff, towards the door.

'When you return? Where will you be?'

He paused, his tall, imposing body swivelling towards where I sat, frozen. 'In Athens, where my business is, and where I intend to stay for the foreseeable future.'

Despite sensing this had been coming, I found the announcement took me by surprise. 'You're leaving me here on my own?'

Theos—could I sound any more alarmed?

He gave a curt, unfeeling nod. 'It is the best decision.'

I pushed my chair back and stood, feeling a yearning spiralling inside that wouldn't be silenced. A yearning to know that his condemnation of my father meant that he was different. That, despite tarring me with the same brush as my parent, he wouldn't punish me too.

'Why can't I live in Athens too?' *With you.*

It would be the perfect place finally to put my art degree to good use. To start a career.

His hardening features broadcasted his displeasure at that question even before he spoke. 'Why force us to endure one another when we don't have to?'

'I'm perfectly happy living on my own. I can rent a flat, get a job in an art gallery—'

The twist of his lips reminded me again of how hot his kisses could be. 'What's the point of staging an elaborate wedding to fool the world if my wife immediately moves into an apartment?'

'Then why did you do it?' I challenged.

'Your father timed his strike to perfection—because my company needs stability now more than ever.'

Invisible walls closed in on me. 'So this is a *business* decision?'

His jaw clenched. '*Everything* that has transpired between us has been based on a business decision.'

Even last night?

My heart lurched and I was glad I was sitting down. 'There has to be another way.'

'There is. You stay here, in our purportedly happy home. You'll want for nothing. Your every wish will be catered for. Buy as much art as you wish to—or even make it if you want.'

Yesterday the promise of freedom from this nightmare would have brought boundless relief. Today, all I felt was…trapped.

'I can't. I can't live like that.'

The words were uttered more for myself than for him. Born from my deep desire never to fall under another's command the way my father had forced me to live under his.

'How long am I to stay in this gilded *prison*?'

His eyes darkened. 'If this is a prison, *yineka mou*, it is not of my making. I tried for months to make your father listen to reason. *He* caused this situation, not me. If you want a way out of this, then find one.'

With that, he walked out, leaving my insides cold as ice.

Axios's words echoed through the long days and nights that followed his departure from Agistros. Long after the days in the luxurious paradise had begun to stretch in brain-numbing monotony.

My new husband, having made his feelings clear about our forced marriage, didn't bother to come home. The stunning villa had indeed become my prison, and its elegant walls and priceless furnishings closed in on me more with every day that dragged by.

And the more my world became narrow, the louder my mother's words and the contents of my grandmother's letter clamoured.

By the end of the second week dejection had me in a constricting hold. But alongside it was the discomfort in my abdomen, which wouldn't let up. Telling myself it was a psychosomatic reaction to my current situation began to feel hollow when I knew my grandmother had felt similar symptoms in the year before her death.

Then the housekeeper informed me one sun-drenched morning that Axios had left a message to say that he would be away on business in New York for another ten days. It seemed like the ominous catalyst I needed.

In the privacy of my suite, I quickly considered and discarded the things I wouldn't need. My large hobo bag was big enough to hold the most crucial essentials, and the small stash of cash I'd saved from my allowance was more than enough to see me through the first few days of my unknown adventure.

After that...

My heart lurched as I attempted to hold down my breakfast the next morning. I took my time, ensuring I was well-sustained before I left the table. Aware of the housekeeper's keen eye, I calmly drank another cup of tea, then helped myself to fruit before drawing back my chair.

'Agatha, I'm thinking of visiting friends. I'm not sure how long I'll be. A few days—maybe longer.'

Surprise lit the housekeeper's eyes. 'But Kyrios Xenakis said you were to stay here—'

'Kyrios Xenakis isn't here. And he's not coming back for ten days. I seriously doubt he'll miss my absence in the meantime.' I slapped on a smile to take the sting out of my words.

She gave a wary nod. 'When do you wish to leave? I'll tell Spiros to ready the boat.'

'Don't bother. I'll grab a water taxi from the harbour. The walk down will do me good.'

Disapproval filmed her eyes. '*Kyria*, I don't think that's a good idea.'

One of the few facts I'd learned about my absent husband was that he was far wealthier than I'd imagined. The members of the Xenakis dynasty basked in the sort of wealth that required bodyguards and well-orchestrated security for them to travel. Exactly the sort of attention I didn't need.

'I appreciate your concern, but it's not necessary, Agatha. Thank you.'

I walked away before she could respond. And, since I wasn't entirely sure she wouldn't alert Axios at the very first opportunity, I rushed up to my suite, grabbed my bag and hurried back down.

Two hours later I stepped up to the sales counter at the airport on the mainland. 'One-way ticket to Switzerland, please.'

The attendant eyed me for what seemed like for ever before issuing my ticket. But if I thought that was nerve-racking, discovering what my grandmother had left for me once I arrived at the Swiss bank left me shamelessly sobbing in a cold and grey bank vault.

And then everything that had gone before paled in comparison to the fear that gripped my heart when I sat before a Swiss doctor three days later.

Dr Trudeau, a short, grey-haired physician with kind eyes, peered at me over his rimless glasses, gentle fingers tapping the file in front of him before he sighed.

'Miss Petras, I have good news and bad news. Although I'm not entirely sure how welcome the good news will be once I explain what I believe is happening with you. I'm so sorry.'

CHAPTER FOUR

One year later

THE TURQUOISE WATERS of the Pacific were so blindingly beautiful they brought tears to my eyes. Or perhaps it was the stinging salt from the spray.

It definitely wasn't because today was my first wedding anniversary.

No. Most certainly not that.

On the list of the most forgettable things to happen to me in the last year, my hastily arranged wedding and the shockingly cold ceremony was right at the top. Not to mention the trapped groom who couldn't wait to walk away from me. The man I now had the dubious pleasure of calling my husband.

My heart leapt into my throat even as I pushed Axios's image away. He would need to be dealt with soon.

But not just yet.

I lifted my face to the blazing sun, willed it to pierce through my desolation and touch my wounded soul. I needed brightness and mirth, sunshine and positivity. If only for a little while longer... It might all be gone soon, slipping through my fingers like mercury.

Gripping the railing of the sleek sailboat transporting me from an exclusive Bora Bora resort to the adjoining uninhabited island where I'd ordered my picnic, I mentally went through my list from bottom to top.

Number five: Take control of my life. *Check.*

Contrary to my fears, walking away hadn't doomed me or my mother. My monthly phone calls reassured me that she was fine. My father, now a hundred million euros richer, was engrossed in yet another business venture. Better still, he hadn't challenged any of the terms of the contract he'd made with Axios.

Number four: Do something worthwhile with my painting. *Check.*

The past year had been frightening in some ways but immensely fulfilling in the exploration of my talent. I was still basking in the knowledge that I could have had a career if fate hadn't pushed me down a different path.

Number three: Accept that my condition might not have a happy ending and that my prognosis might follow my grandmother's. *Check.*

It had been a difficult acceptance, often pitted with tears and heartache and grief for all the things I might never have. For what this would do to those I love.

Number two: Cherish my precious gift for as long as I can. *Check. Check. Check.*

The last item on my list filled me with equal parts desolation and trepidation. But it needed to be done.

Number one: Hand over my precious gift to Axios Xenakis.

As if that gift knew he was in my thoughts, a soft cry rippled through the sun-drenched breeze, followed by a sharper one, demanding attention.

Smiling, I turned from the railing and crossed the deck to the shaded lounge. There, lying amongst the cushions, was the reason for my heartbeat. The reason I needed to keep fighting for my unknown future.

'Are you awake, my precious boy?'

At the sound of my voice Andreos Xenakis kicked his plump legs, his arms joining in his giddy response as his searching eyes found mine. For an instant my breath caught. The similarity between the piercing grey eyes of father and son was so visceral, I froze.

Another insistent cry had me reaching for him. His warm, solid weight in my arms quieted the worst of my trepidation, and soon even that evaporated beneath the sheer joy of cradling him, feeding him, doing such mundane things as changing his nappy and handing him his favourite toy, basking in his sweet babbling while I enjoyed the stunning view and just...*being*.

Pushing away the terrifying news the doctor had given me that day in Switzerland and the choice I'd had to make, I breathed in relief when the boat slowed and a staff member approached with a courteous smile.

'We're here, miss. Your picnic is set up for you on the shore.'

Whatever the future held, I would deal with it.

After all, I'd dealt with so much this past year.

Except the future had found me before I was ready. And it came in the form of a solitary figure with furious gunmetal eyes and a gladiator stance, waiting with crossed arms on the jetty as the sailboat returned to the exclusive resort.

My heart leapt into my throat, my breath strangled to nothing as I watched the figure grow larger, more broody, more formidable.

More everything.

He'd grown harder. Edgier. Or perhaps that was all imagined. A product of those feverishly erotic dreams that frequently plagued me.

Whatever... The man who watched me in silent condemnation as the boat gently butted the wooden planks on the jetty had zero mercy in him. And when his gaze shifted to Andreos and widened with chilled shock I had the distinct notion that I'd played this wrong.

I'd been too selfish.

Taken too much time for myself.

Too much time with my son.

'Axios.'

He didn't respond to my whispered utterance of his name. He couldn't take his eyes off Andreos. His strong throat moved in a swallow and his pallor increased as several expressions charged through his eyes.

Shock. Amazement. Utter fury.

'What are you doing here?' I asked.

Finally eyes the colour of a dark arctic night clashed with mine. 'What am I *doing* here?' he asked with icy incredulity. 'This is what you have to say to me after the stunt you have pulled?'

My insides shook but I forced myself to hold his gaze. 'You'll want to discuss this, I'm sure, but can it wait till—?'

'I'll *want to discuss this*? Are you for real?'

A drowsy Andreos stirred in my arms, his senses picking up on the frenetic emotions charging through the air.

'Miss, would you like us to—?'

'Leave us.' Axios's tone was deep. Implacable.

I wasn't in the least bit surprised when the staff hurried away.

'How did you find me?'

It seemed a monumental feat for him to drag his gaze from Andreos.

'Through an act of sheer coincidence. The owner of this resort happens to be a business acquaintance of mine. He was on a rare tour of his property when he spotted you. Had he not chosen to take his yearly tour this last week...' He stopped, shaking his head as if grappling with the sheer serendipity of the occurrence that had led him to me.

My chalet was on the beach, and I made the short walk to the gorgeous timber-clad structure aware of his every step behind me.

'I intended to come back—I promise.'

'You *promise*? Why should I take your word on anything? You told the staff you were visiting friends when all along you intended to abscond from our marriage. And now you're hiding in a resort on the other side of the world under a false name. Not to mention you seem to have had a child during that time. I am assuming the child is yours?'

'Of course he his. Who else's would he be?'

He went as rigid as an ice statue, and what little colour had flowed back into his face on the walk from jetty to chalet receded momentarily before fury reddened his haughty cheekbones once more.

'So I can add infidelity to your sins?'

'Infid—? What are you talking about?' Shock made my voice screech.

Andreos whimpered as I laid him down in his cot, and then went back to sound sleep.

'We used contraception on our wedding night, as I recall,' he rasped with icy condemnation.

'Well, I wasn't on birth control. I never have been. And, while I'm not an expert, I'm sure there's a caution that states that condoms aren't one hundred percent foolproof.'

'And I'm suddenly to accept that the protection that has never failed me before suddenly malfunctioned with *you*?'

I wasn't sure why the reference to other lovers drilled such angst through me. His lovers, past or present, were of no consequence to me. I had no hold over him, nor did he over me, when it came right down to it. All that had brought us together was my father's greed and manipulation.

'I don't know what to say to make you believe me but I know the truth, Axios. Andreos is yours.'

Piercing eyes locked on mine for the better part

of a minute. 'If he's mine, why have you hidden him from me for the better part of a year?'

His voice had changed, turned grittier, and he even looked a little shaken as his gaze swung again to Andreos. He started to walk towards the cot as if compelled, then stopped, shook his head.

'Why is he here on the other side of the world when he should be in Greece, with his family?'

It would have been so easy to blurt out everything that had happened to me since that dreaded visit to the doctor in Switzerland. and the urgent summons to hear my diagnosis three gut-churning days later, when it had been confirmed that there was indeed a growth in my cervix.

But I was also told I was pregnant, and that any further exploration, even an initial biopsy to ascertain its malignancy or benignity, would jeopardise my baby.

I could have told him about the latest scans I had in my suitcase, taken by Dr Trudeau in Switzerland, and his recommendation to take action.

But if Axios's presence here wasn't warning enough that the time I'd bought for myself was over, the look in his eyes said I wouldn't escape scot-free.

Nevertheless, I wasn't the same woman he'd

married. Harrowing decisions made in the cold grip of fear had a way of changing a person.

'Why does it matter to you, anyway? I thought you would be glad to see the back of me for ever.'

A ferocious light glinted in his eyes for a heart-stopping second before he took a step towards me. 'You married a Xenakis, Calypso. You think simply packing your bag and walking out through the door is the end of it? That you simply had to hightail it to the other end of the world for your marriage vows to cease to have meaning?'

I stemmed my panic as his words rankled. 'Our vows had *meaning*? I could've sworn you challenged me to find a way to make them *stop* having meaning.'

His eyes narrowed. 'You think *this* was the answer?'

'It was *my* way!'

'Perhaps I should've added an addendum that finding a way needed to involve discretion and consideration. Nothing that would throw a spotlight on me or my family. My mistake. Tell me, Calypso, do you think disappearing off the face of the earth for over a year screams discretion or consideration?'

I shrugged with a carelessness I didn't feel. 'You didn't stick around long enough to hash out another course of action. I did what was best.'

'What was best for *you*, you mean?'

My senses wanted to scream *yes!* Caution warned me to remain calm. To talk this through as rationally as the tower of formidable fury in front of me would allow.

'You still haven't told me why you're here.'

He made another sound of incredulity. 'Because you're my wife! Because the whispers need to cease. Because you will not jeopardise everything I've worked for. And that's just for starters.'

'Ah, *now* we're getting to the bottom of it. You're here because of what my absence is doing to your business? Is that it, Axios?'

With lightning speed warm fingers curled over my nape. His hold wasn't threatening, simply holding me in place so that whatever point he needed to make would be accurately delivered.

'While no one would dare say it to my face, rumours of my wife fleeing our marital home has caused ripples in my life. The kind I can do without. So make no mistake: I intend to remedy that. Whatever point you intended to make, it ends now.'

Each word contained a deadly promise—an intention to have his way that stoked the rebellion that had gone dormant in the last year back to life.

'Believe it or not, my walking out had absolutely nothing to do with you.'

'Enlighten me, then, *matia mou*. What was it all about?'

The soft cadence of his voice didn't fool me.

'What could possibly have driven you from the life of luxury and abundance your father battled for so cunningly?'

The mention of my father brought my goals back into focus. Reminded me why I hadn't been able to stomach staying under Axios's roof for one more day. That feeling of a loss of control. Of suffocation. Of not being able to live my life on my own terms. My choices being taken away from me without so much as a by your leave…

'I'm not my father,' I stressed, with every cell in my body.

'No, you're not. But while I was prepared to give you the benefit of the doubt before, your actions have led me to form a different opinion about you. So whatever your reasons were, tell me now.'

'Or what?'

He didn't speak for the longest moment. Then his attention shifted to the cot where Andreos slept, lost in baby dreams. My heart tripped over itself as I watched Axios's face. Watched him

speculate with that clever mind financial ana-
lysts rhapsodised over.

'Is he the reason?'

'What do you mean?'

His jaw rippled. 'If there was an indiscretion,
I urge you to confess it now rather than later.'

His words shouldn't have scraped my emotions. Considering what my mother had done,
and the fall-out and gossip that had followed, I
knew all too well how assumptions were made,
judgements passed without verification. But the
reality that he suspected Andreos wasn't his
lanced a soft spot in my heart.

A fierce need to protect my child's honour
ploughed through me. 'We may not have known
each other before we met at the altar, but you
should know that I would rather cut off my own
arm before attempting to lie about my child's
parentage. Whether you're willing to accept it
or not, he's yours.'

If I'd expected my fervour to melt his coldness,
I was sorely disappointed.

'Your vigorous defence of your child is admi-
rable. But, as you said, we were virtual strangers before we came together. If you want me to
believe you, tell me where you've been. Every
single thing you've done in the past year. Then
perhaps I'll consider believing you.'

The list reeled through my head.

Finding the bank account in Switzerland my grandmother had left in my name.

Seeing the private doctor who'd treated me.

Getting the results and feeling the soul-wrecking fear that my fate would echo my grandmother's.

Making the choice I had to make.

Andreos's arrival.

Saying the fervent prayers for *more*. One more day. One week. One month.

One year.

I couldn't tell Axios any of that. Even the simple joy of rediscovering my love of painting and finding the shops and galleries I'd sold my watercolours to seemed too sacred, too private to share with the man who looked at me with rancour and suspicion. Whose every breath seemed like a silent pledge to uncover my secrets.

My life. Lived on my terms.

That was what I'd sworn to myself that rainy afternoon in my hotel room after leaving Dr Trudeau's office. For the most part, it had been.

Axios's arrival had simply shortened the time I'd given myself before checking off the last item on my list.

'You'll consider believing me after you've triple-checked everything I say?'

The unapologetic gleam in his eyes told me he intended to do exactly that. Tear through every new, unconditional friendship I'd formed along the way, every haven I'd sought refuge in.

My stomach churned at the thought of Axios finding out the true state of my health and exploiting it the way my father had done with my mother. It was that terrible thought more than anything else that cemented my decision to keep my secret.

If he found out my condition, he would wonder if the state of my health affected my suitability as a mother. Unlike my mother, my flaws weren't outward. For the precious time being, I could hang on to that.

As for when I couldn't…

'All you need to know is that Andreos is yours and I'm prepared to return to Greece. If that's what you want?'

His nostrils flared and his gaze raked my face for long sizzling seconds before his lips twisted. 'Oh, yes, wife. The time has most definitely come for that. And whatever it is that you're keeping from me, rest assured, I'll find out.'

With that he stepped back.

Thinking he was going to leave me to grapple with the turmoil his unexpected arrival had caused, I watched, my heart speeding like a

freight train, as he headed to the cot where Andreos slept.

Silence disturbed only by the slow stirring of
the ceiling fan throbbed in the room as Axios
stared down at the son he hadn't accepted was
his. His jaw clenched tight and his throat moved
convulsively as he watched the rise and fall of
the baby's chest.

He remained frozen for so long I feared he'd
take root there. When he turned abruptly and
tugged a sleek phone from his pocket my senses
tripped.

'What are you doing?'

Eyes the colour of a stormy sky met mine as
he hit a number and lifted the handset to his ear.
'Getting the answers I need.'

The sharp orders he gave in Greek when the
phone was answered didn't surprise me. The
irony that the one truth I'd told him was the one
he was having a hard time accepting wasn't lost
on me. But, conversely, I understood. I too had
wondered why fate would choose to lay both joy
and sorrow on me in one fell swoop, leaving me
with a choice that had seemed both simple and
terrifying.

After all, my actions pointed to behaviour that
would've left *me* suspicious too. And, considering what my own mother had done for the sake

of freedom and love—an act that was an open secret in Nicrete—I didn't blame Axios for wanting to verify that the baby he'd helped create was truly his.

When he was done making an appointment for his private doctor to visit his home in Athens the moment he returned, to take DNA samples for a paternity test, he hung up, his piercing regard staying on me as he tucked his phone away.

I ignored the blatant challenge and asked the question more important to me. 'Is it going to hurt him?'

For the most fleeting second the charged look in his eyes dissipated. 'No. I'm told all it requires is a swab from his cheek.'

I nodded. 'Very well, then.'

He frowned, my easy acquiescence seemingly throwing him. But his face returned to its formidable hauteur in moments, and his strides were purposeful as he strode to the house phone and picked it up.

Before he dialled he turned to me. 'Is the child okay to travel on a plane?'

'The *child's* name is Andreos. And I'd thank you not to make any plans without discussing them with me first.'

A muscle ticked in his jaw. 'Why? Did you not tell me that you intended to return to Greece?'

'Yes, I did.'

'When exactly were you proposing to do that? When he was a year old? When he was five or perhaps ten?' he grated out.

The cold embrace of knowing that time wasn't on my side stalled my answer for several seconds. 'I was thinking days—not months or years. My booking at this resort is only for a week. I was going to fly back to Athens from here.'

His lips flattened. 'I don't plan on leaving you behind, Calypso. My good faith where you're concerned is gone. When I fly out of here in three hours you and the child will be by my side. And that state will continue until such time as you choose to come completely clean about your actions for the past year or I furnish myself with the information.'

After that, there really wasn't much more to say.

Moments after Axios left my suite the head concierge arrived with instructions to get as many staff as I needed to help me pack. I almost laughed, considering my meagre belongings and everything Andreos needed could fit in one small suitcase.

I dismissed the staff and was done with my packing in twenty minutes. The rest of the time I spent sitting beside Andreos's cot, hoping against hope that my time with him going forward would be just as peaceful as the past precious months had been. Because I didn't intend to be separated from him for a second. Time was too precious. Too special. And I would fight for every moment.

As if aware he was at the centre of my thoughts, he stirred and woke, his face remaining solemn for a few seconds before a toothless smile creased his chubby face. Blinking back the tears of joy that just looking at him prompted, I scooped him up and cradled him close.

By the time Axios knocked on the door we were both ready.

After another taut spell of staring at Andreos with turbulent eyes, he eyed the single suitcase with grating consternation. 'This is all you have?'

'I believe in travelling light.'

His expression darkened. 'What about safety equipment for the baby? A car seat?'

'I find it easier to hire what I require as and when I need it. And, before you disparage my methods, I research and make sure everything I use is of the highest safety standard.'

His gaze remained on me for another second before he nodded at the porter.

My suitcase was quickly stowed on a sleek private boat. Within minutes my last sanctuary had become a dot on the horizon.

I'd forgotten just how ruthlessly efficient Axios Xenakis could be. I received another rude reminder when, upon our arrival at the jetty, a smiling courier presented me with a gleaming state-of-the-art buggy and car seat combo, already assembled.

I braced my hand on Andreos's back, tugged him closer to where he nestled snugly in his papoose. 'That won't be necessary. The airline I'm flying with will have all the equipment I need.'

Axios stepped forward and took hold of the pushchair. 'You think I'm going to let you out of my sight now I've found you?'

'But I have a ticket—'

'And I have a private jet.'

Of course he did.

I'd blocked so many things out of my mind for the sake of pure survival. But the world had kept on turning. Axios had remained a powerful mogul with looks that weakened women's knees. And, as a billionaire who commanded an airline empire, didn't it stand to reason he'd possess his own plane?

A short SUV ride later we arrived at the private area of the airport, where an obscenely large aircraft bearing the unique Xenakis family logo stood gleaming resplendently beneath the French Polynesian sun.

'So what's it to be? Athens or Agistros?' he asked silkily.

I stared at him in surprise. 'You're giving me a *choice*?' It was more than he had the last time. More than my father ever had. Not that I planned on reading anything into it.

He shrugged. 'The location doesn't matter. Whichever you choose will be home. *For all of us,*' he added succinctly.

I chose Athens.

A mere twenty-four hours later we drove through the imposing gates of Axios's jaw-dropping villa. A different set of staff greeted us, and an even more opulent set of adjoining master suites had been readied for the prodigal wife's return.

I was standing in the middle of cream and gold opulence when I felt his presence behind me. Not wanting to look into those hypnotising eyes, I kept still, my precious bundle safely tucked in my arms.

My skin beginning to tingle wildly, I snatched in a breath and held it when his mouth brushed over the shell of my ear and he said, in a low, deep whisper, 'Welcome home, *yineka mou.* And rest assured that this time you will not get away from me that easily.'

CHAPTER FIVE

MY SON.

I have a son.

My chest squeezed tight. The emotions tumbling through me were…indescribable.

Back on Bora Bora everything inside me had prompted me to accept Calypso at her word—accept that the child was mine. Only I'd made the mistake before of thinking I could manage her, that she was a victim when she was anything but. She was cunning. Intelligent and resourceful enough to disappear without a trace for a whole year.

And apparently to take what is mine with her.

The result of the paternity test spelled out in stark indelible ink confirmed that, in this at least, Calypso had spoken the truth. But swiftly on the heels of that knowledge came a mystifying mix of searing fury and heady delight—the former for what I'd been deprived of and the latter for the astounding gift I hadn't even realised I wanted.

My son.

She kept him from me. Deliberately. Chose to leave my home and have my baby on her own, with no care as to what my feelings were in the matter. Why? Because I'd left her on Agistros? In the lap of the kind of luxury most people only dreamed about?

But did you give her any choice?

I swallowed the bite of guilt as my eyes locked on the paper.

Andreos.

Even as a part of my brain tested the name out and accepted that it fitted him my fingers were shaking with the enormity of everything I'd missed. Things I'd never have thought would matter suddenly assumed colossal importance.

His first cry.

His first smile.

His first laugh...

Did babies his age laugh? I'd been robbed of the opportunity to find out for myself.

I tossed the document away and stood. Sudden weakness in my legs stopped me from moving. One hand braced on the polished wood surface, I sucked in a deep breath, attempted to bring myself under control.

Control was essential. Over my erratic emotions. Over my wayward wife and over the belief that she should take such actions without consequence. To deprive me of my own flesh and blood…

Why?

The deeply visceral need to know straightened my spine.

I found her in the smallest living room—the room farthest from my study and the one she seemed to have commandeered for herself and Andreos since her return. He lay on a mat on the floor, his fists and legs pumping with abandon as Calypso crouched over him. A few toys were strewn nearby, momentarily forgotten as mother and son indulged in a staring game of some sort. One that amused Andreos…*my son.*

So babies his age did smile. They also returned their mother's stare with rapt attention until they were tickled, then dissolved into heaps of laughter.

Something stirred raw and powerful within me as I stared into the eyes that had seemed familiar to me from the start, even as I cautioned myself against full acceptance. The feeling intensified as I watched Calypso's utter devotion, saw the bond between mother and son, the unit I'd been excluded from.

The unit I wanted to belong to—

Sensing my presence, Calypso's gaze flew to mine, then immediately shadowed.

Theos mou, was I really that frightful?

'You can be.'

I dismissed the uncanny sound of Neo's voice in my head.

Too bad. I'd given her four days to settle in. Four days of swimming in the uncharted waters of her re-entry into my life with a son...*my son*...in tow.

It took me but a moment to summon Sophia, one of several household staff who'd been infatuated with Andreos since his arrival.

To Calypso, I said, 'We need to talk. Come with me. Sophia will look after Andreos.'

Her clear reluctance lasted for the moment it took for her to spot the piece of paper clutched in my fist. Then she slowly rose.

About to head back to my study, I changed my mind and headed up the stairs.

'Where are we going?'

The hint of nervousness in her voice rankled further.

'Where we won't be disturbed,' I replied as evenly as I could manage.

'But...'

I stopped and turned. 'Do you have a problem with being alone with me?'

The faintest flush crept into her cheeks, but her head remained high, her gaze bold. 'Of course not.'

Truth be told, perhaps my suite wasn't the best choice. Amongst everything I'd imagined might happen when I finally located my wayward wife, discovering that the chemistry that had set us aflame on our wedding night still blazed with unrelenting power was the last thing I'd expected.

The fact that I couldn't look at the curve of her delicate jaw without imagining trailing my lips over her smooth skin, tasting the vitality of the pulse that beat at her throat or palming her now even more ample breasts was an unwelcome annoyance that nevertheless didn't stop my mind from wandering where it shouldn't.

Did unfettered pleasure still overtake her in that sizzling, unique way it had during our one coming together? Did she go out of her head with unbridled passion at the merest touch? If so, just who had been stoking that particular flame in her year-long absence?

It took every ounce of control I had to contain my searing jealousy at the thought. Answers to those questions would come later. *This* was too important.

Without stopping to further examine the wisdom of the venue, I made my way into the room.

She followed, making a point to avoid looking at the bed as she passed through into the private living room. From my position before the fireplace I watched her take a seat and neatly fold her hands in her lap. Had her pulse not been racing in her throat I would have been fooled by her complete serenity.

'He's mine.'

Just saying the words dragged earth-shaking emotion through me, robbing me of my next breath. That a small bundle could do that—

'I told you he was.'

There was a new defiance in her demeanour, a quiet, fiery strength that had been there a year ago but had matured now.

'I've never lied to you.'

'Then what do you call *this*?' I tossed the report on the coffee table.

She paled a little, her throat moving in another swallow. And why did I find that simple evidence that she felt *something* so riveting?

'You were always going to know your son, Axios. I simply took a little time before informing you.'

Rejection seared deep. 'No. I should've been

informed the moment you found out you were carrying my child.'

'Why? So we could discuss it like a *loving married couple*? Or so you could treat it as another *business* transaction, like our arranged marriage? I'm sure you'll forgive me for choosing neither option, since the former was a farce and the latter was unpalatable.'

The accusation scored a direct hit, making my neck heat with another trace of guilt. Over the last year I'd gone over everything that had happened in those twenty-four hours. Accepted that perhaps I could've handled things differently. But was this the price I had to pay for it?

'I had a right to know, Calypso.' My voice emerged much gruffer than I'd intended. And deep inside me something like sorrow turned over.

Her lashes swept down, but not before I spotted the sea of turmoil swelling in the blue depths. My nape tightened and my instincts blared with the notion that she was hiding something.

'What if I told you that I didn't know what I wanted?' she asked.

A white-hot knife sliced through me at the thought that it would have decimated me had she taken a different route than bearing my son.

'Calypso…'

Her name sounded thick on my tongue. I waited until she raised her gaze to mine.

'Yes?'

'Regardless of this…disagreement between us, you will have my gratitude for choosing to carry our son for ever.'

Her eyes widened in stunned surprise. 'Um… you're welcome,' she murmured.

Once again her gaze swept away from mine— a small gesture that disturbed and confounded me. And then that defiant bolt of blue clashed with mine and absurd anticipation simmered in my gut.

'He's here now. Can we not put what has gone on in the past behind us and move on?'

'Certainly we can. As soon as you tell me what I want to know I'll take great strides to put it all behind me.'

Again that mutinous look took her over, sparking my own need to tangle with it. To stoke her fire until we both burned.

'Are you prepared to do that, Calypso?'

For several moments she held my gaze. Breath stalled, I awaited an answer…*one* answer…to quell the questions teeming inside me. But then that unnerving serenity settled on her face again.

'It's not important—'

'*Not important?* You leave my home under

cover of a blatant falsehood, then you disappear for a year, during which time you bear my son, and you think your absence isn't *important*?'

'Careful, Axios, or I'll be inclined to wonder whether you actually missed the wife you bothered with for less than a day before walking away.'

I sucked in a stunned breath. A year ago she'd warned me that she wouldn't be biddable. Discovering she was innocent had clouded that warning. But this kitten had well and truly developed claws. Sharp ones. I was tempted to test them. Intellectually and...yes...*physically*.

Unbidden, heat throbbed deep in my groin, stirring desires I'd believed were long dead until one glimpse of my wayward wife from a jetty in Bora Bora had fiercely reawakened them.

That unholy union of sexual tension and unanswered questions propelled me to where she sat, cloaked in secrets that mocked me.

Her slight tensing when I crouched in front of her unsettled me further, despite the fact that I should've been satisfied to see that she wasn't wholly indifferent to me.

'You want to know about the inconvenience your absence caused, Calypso?'

She remained silent.

'Some newspaper hack got wind that my wife

wasn't in Agistros, enjoying her first weeks of marital bliss. Nor was she with friends, as she'd led everyone to believe. To all intents and purposes she seemed to have fallen off the face of the earth.'

A delicate frown creased her brows. 'Why would that be of interest to anyone? Especially when you intended to banish me to Agistros for the duration of our arrangement anyway?'

'You're my wife. Everything you do is news. And appearing to have deserted your marriage was definitely newsworthy.'

She blinked. '*Appearing* to have?'

'I have an outstanding PR team who've had to work tirelessly to put a lid on this.'

There was no hint of remorse on her sun-kissed face. Instead she looked irritated. 'If you've managed to somehow spin my absence to suit our narrative then there's no problem, is there?'

I allowed myself a small smile, one her gaze clung to with wary eyes. 'You would like that, wouldn't you? To escape every unpleasant fallout from your actions?'

'You don't have the first idea of what I want, Axios.'

My name on her lips sent a punch of heat through me. Thinking back, I couldn't recollect her ever saying it before Bora Bora. Not when she'd spat fire at me, not when she'd confessed her untouched state, and not when she'd been in the complete grip of passion. Certainly not when she'd asked me to take her with me to Athens.

There had been far too many times over the last year when I'd regretted not doing so—not because of that infernal hunger that had long outstayed its welcome, but simply because it would have curtailed her actions.

But the past was the past. There was still the future to deal with. And my new reality.

My son.

'For the sake of probability, and if I were in the mood to grant wishes, what exactly would you want, *matia mou*?'

Wariness made her hesitate, but slowly defiance laced with something else pushed through. 'I'd want a divorce. As soon as possible.'

Stunned disbelief rose in me like a monumental wave I'd once ridden on the North Shore, and then just as swiftly crashed on the beach of her sheer audacity and shock. It was all so very dramatic.

I couldn't help it. I laughed.

Her pert little nose quivered as she inhaled sharply. 'What's so funny?'

Affront and defiance flushed her skin a sweet pink, drawing my attention to her alluring features. My wife was now all woman. An arrestingly feminine woman who'd just demanded...*a divorce.*

'Why you, my dear, and your continued ability to surprise me.'

'I'm glad you're amused. But I'm deadly serious. I want a divorce.'

Humour evaporated as abruptly as it had arrived. Leaning forward, I grasped her upper arms and fought not to be distracted by her smooth supple skin or the need to caress her and reacquaint myself with her.

My once sound argument about staying away from her had backfired spectacularly. I'd left her on Agistros thinking that she'd be safe and I'd be saved from temptation. Look how that had turned out.

Even with sex off the table I should have kept her close. I could have prevented her fleeing. Instead I'd borne the subtle snipes of those who had been quick to point out my failure. Quick to compare me to my grandfather and test me to see whether I'd crack under the same pressure.

With Calypso gone I'd experienced a taste of what he'd gone through—sometimes even with members of my own family.

Now she was back...and asking for a divorce.

'We seem to have veered a little off-track to

be indulging in hypotheticals. You'll recall that, according to the agreement, this marriage needs to last at least twelve months.'

'Yes, I remember.'

'Twelve *ongoing* months. Not twelve absentee months.'

She swallowed and my fingers moved, some compulsion driving me to glide my fingers up her neck, trace the colour flowing back into her cheeks. She made a sound under her breath, bearing a hint of those she'd made on our wedding night.

Before I could revel in it she pulled back abruptly. My hands dropped back to her arms.

'My father hasn't contested the agreement,' she said.

'So you took the time to check on his activities?' Disgruntlement rumbled through me at the thought.

Her flush gave me my answer. 'What are you saying, Axios?'

'I'm saying the clock stopped the moment you walked out. But, fortunately for you, your father is no longer in the picture. For one thing he can't prove that you've been an absentee wife—unless you apprised him of your intentions?'

'No, I didn't,' she muttered, her eyes not quite meeting mine.

I'd long suspected that while she might have avoided contact with her father, her mother was a different story. But Iona Petras had remained resolutely closed-lipped about the whereabouts of her daughter.

'Good—then the ball, as they say, is in my court.'

She met my gaze boldly, read my clear intent and gasped. 'You mean you have the power to give me a divorce but...?' Her voice dried up, a telling little shiver racing through her body.

'But I won't, sweet Calypso. Not until a few things are set straight.'

'What things?'

'For starters, my PR company didn't make *all* the problems go away. While I frustrated the news media enough to make them chase other headlines, my competitors and my business partners were another story. Your absence fuelled enough rumours about instability to stall my latest deal.'

A peculiar expression that resembled hurt crossed her face. 'So this is about stocks and shares again?'

The disparaging note in her voice grated. 'Why? Did you want it to be something more?'

She stiffened. 'No.'

Her firm, swift denial rankled, but again I dismissed it. 'There will be no divorce. Not until I'm completely satisfied that there will be no permanent fall-out from your actions. And not until we've thoroughly discussed the impact this will have on Andreos.'

She stiffened. 'Does it occur to you that I might be doing this for him? That this arrangement might not be the best environment for him?'

'Then we will strive to make it so. You'll get your divorce, if you wish it. It could be as early as a month from now or it could be the year you were supposed to give me. In that time, wherever I go, you and my son will go also. He will be your priority. But when called upon you will be at my side at public functions and you will play the role of a devoted wife. And you will do all of that without the smallest hint that there's dissent between us.'

Her sweet, stubborn chin lifted in a clear defiance. 'And if I don't? What's to stop me giving the newspapers what they want? Telling them the true state of this so-called marriage?'

Why did her rebellion fire me up so readily? In truth, very few people got to display such attitude towards me. Neo tried me at the best of times, but even he knew when to back down. The rest of my family fell in line, because ultimately I held the purse strings.

But it seemed my errant wife's fiery spirit turned me on. Made me want to burn in the fire of it.

I caught her chin in my hand, my thumb moving almost of its own volition to slide over the dark rose swell of her lower lip. She shivered, this time unable to disguise her arousal. I intensified the caress, a little too eager to see how far she was truly affected. Blue eyes held mine for another handful of seconds before they dropped. But her breathing grew more erratic, her pulse hammering against the silken skin of her throat.

I held still, my groin rudely awakening as the little eddy of lust whipped faster, threatened to turn into a cyclone.

'You really wish to defy me? You think that now you and your family have received what they want they can simply sit back and enjoy the spoils of their ill-gotten gains? Do you think that I will let you get away with it?'

She glared blue fire at me. 'I won't be ordered about, Axios. I won't be dictated to like one of your minions!'

'I would never mistake you for a minion. But a little hellcat, intent on sinking her claws into me? Definitely.'

For a charged moment she returned my stare. Then her gaze dropped to my lips.

A sort of madness took over. A breathless second later our lips met in a fiery clash, the hot little gasp she gave granting me access to the sharp tongue that seemed intent on creating havoc with my mood and my libido.

Caught in the grip of hunger, I slicked my tongue against hers, took hold of one hip to hold her in place. She attempted to smother her moan, attempted not to squirm with the arousal I could already sense. I needed more. Needed confirmation of...*something*. Something that bore a hint of the torrid dreams that had plagued me almost nightly for a solid year. Something to take away the disarming hollowness that had resided in me since I'd got the call in New York that my wife had fled Agistros.

My teeth grazed the tip of her tongue when it attempted to issue a challenge. This time she couldn't hold back her moan. Couldn't stop herself from straining against me, from gasping her need.

And when she did I took. Savoured. Then devoured.

Her moans fuelled my desire, and the scramble of her hands over my chest, then around to my back facilitated the urgent need to lay her on the sofa so I could slide over her, to once again experience the heady sensation of having Calypso beneath me.

Her nails dug in deeper as I lowered myself over her, felt the heavy swell of her breasts press again my chest. The recollection that she'd borne my child, that she still nurtured him, was a powerful aphrodisiac that charged through me and hardened me in the most profoundly carnal way.

Could I get any more primitive?

Yes, my senses screamed.

The deepening urge to claim and keep what was mine thundered harder through me, drawing me away from the naked temptation of her lips to the seductive smoothness of her throat, her vibrant pulse, the exquisite valley between her breasts.

It took but a moment to slide the thin sleeve of her sundress off her shoulder, to release the front clasp and nudge aside the cup of her bra to bare her delicious flesh to my ravenous gaze. To mould the plump mound in anticipation of drawing that stiff, rosy peak into my mouth.

Beneath me, Calypso's breath caught. Her eyes turned a dark blue with the same fiery lust that was causing carnage wit in me, then snapped to mine and stayed there.

Slowly, with an ultra-feminine arching of her back that held me deeply enthralled, she offered herself to me, somehow turning the tables on me. Because for all that this was supposed to be a punitive lesson, a way to remind her who held the power now, after her actions had swung the tide to my advantage, I was caught in a vortex of desire so voracious I couldn't have stopped even if I'd wanted to.

So I lowered my head and with a powerless groan sucked the bud into my mouth.

Savage hunger exploded inside me, all my senses lost as her fingers locked in my hair and held me to my delightful task.

'Oh... *Theos mou*,' she gasped.

The memory of our one night together, of her unreserved responsiveness and the unique way she'd expressed her pleasure, sharpened my hunger, sparking a desire to relive that experience. I slid one hand beneath her body, urged her even closer. She answered by arching higher, offering more of herself to me.

'Tell me what you're feeling,' I urged thickly, aware that my voice was hoarse, barely intelligible.

She froze, the eyes that had rolled shut mere seconds ago flying open.

Watching her, I lazily caught that peak between my teeth, felt a carnal shudder unravel through her. 'You taste exquisite.'

Arousal and denial warred in her face, and then her fingers flew from my hair as small but effective hands pushed at my shoulders. 'No! Stop!'

For a moment I considered a different tactic. Negotiation. Talking her round to my way of thinking. Satisfying this need that dogged us both. But hadn't my family and I given the Petrases enough in this lifetime? This was supposed to be the time to extract *my* pound of flesh after what they'd done to my grandfather. Besides, sex was what had led us here in the first place. Was I really going to fall into the well of temptation I'd counselled myself against a year ago when I should be dealing with the reality of my son?

The reminder was enough to propel me off her and across the room. Even then it took several control-gathering breaths to master my raging libido. It didn't help that her reflection in the window showed her naked breasts for another handful of seconds before she righted her clothes.

When she was done, she rose. She didn't approach—which was a good thing, because I wasn't sure I wouldn't have given in to the urge to finish what we'd started.

'Axios…'

I gritted my teeth, the discovery that my name on her lips was its own special brand of hell driving my fingers through my hair.

This had gone on long enough. 'This is no longer purely business, Calypso. I want to know my son.'

I caught another expression on her face—one that sent a different type of emotion charging through me.

I turned around, wanting to verify it more accurately, but whatever it was had gone, her face a composed mask.

'Of course. I won't stand in the way of that.'

Why didn't that agreement satisfy me?

Why did that hollowness still remain?

'Good. Then we shelve discussion of divorce until further notice.'

That gruff, shaken tone was gone. It was almost as if that little display of emotion over his son had never happened. As if the wild little tumble on the sofa less than five minutes ago was already a distant memory.

But, no…there were tell-tale signs. Signs I didn't want to notice. Like how deliciously tousled his dark, luxuriously wavy hair was now, courtesy of my restless fingers. How colour still rose in his chiselled cheekbones.

And that definitive bulge behind his fly—

With a willpower that threatened to sap the last of my composure I averted my gaze from the pillar of temptation he represented, and reminded myself why we were here in the first place. Dear heaven. I needed to be done with this before the desire I'd believed eroded by distance and absence made a complete fool of me.

'I need your word, Calypso.'

The implacable demand centred my thoughts. Reminded me that this wasn't over. Contrary to what I'd believed, twelve months of living apart from him had done nothing to lessen my sentence. I was back to square one, with a child to think about.

A child Axios fully intended to claim.

'Where exactly does Andreos feature in your grand plan?' I asked, belatedly focusing on the most precious thing in my life. On safeguarding his welfare before I embarked on fighting for my survival.

Axios's head went back, as if the question offended him. 'He is my son. He will be brought up under our care with the full benefit of the Xenakis name at his disposal for as long as he needs it.'

Through all of this I'd held on to the secret fear that Andreos might suffer. Over the past year I'd meticulously researched the Xenakis dynasty, with Andreos's needs at the forefront of my mind.

Outwardly, they appeared a close unit—but, as with most super-wealthy and influential families, rumours of acrimony abounded. Once or twice it had been rumoured that Axios's status as CEO had been challenged by a daring cousin or uncle. None had succeeded, of course.

'You give me your word that you'll protect Andreos, no matter what?'

'Of course. I vow it.' His voice was deep and solemn and immediate.

Relief weakened my knees, and for some absurd reason I wanted to throw my arms around him. 'Thank you.'

His frown deepened, speculation narrowing his eyes. I turned away before he could read my anxiety. Now wasn't the time to think about my precarious health…about the tough road ahead. About the battle my grandmother had fought against cervical cancer and eventually lost.

And it certainly wasn't the time to dwell on the fact that the pain in my abdomen remained, its presence edging into my consciousness with each passing day.

'Possible cancer… Prognosis uncertain if you choose to keep your baby…'

Dr Trudeau's words broke free from the vault I'd kept them in. Along with the frighteningly easy decision I'd made to keep my baby for as long as I could instead of chasing risky surgery. The tearful gratitude for every day Andreos had nestled in my womb, growing despite the unknown threat to his life and mine.

And his sweet cry the moment he was born.

I'd learned quickly that for my son's sake I needed to compartmentalise. His keen intelligence and sensitivity, even at such a tender age, had focused me on giving him my very best—always. But giving him my best included fighting to remain in his life. Even if I had to temporarily entrust him to Axios in order to do so.

'Do you agree?' Axios pressed, his gaze probing mercilessly.

'I'll give you what you want on one condition. Take it or leave it.'

After a moment he jerked his head in command for me to continue.

'I'll stay until your precious deal is done. On condition that you don't attempt to interfere in my relationship with my son.'

'What gives you the impression that I'd wish to do anything of the sort?'

My shrug fell short of full efficiency under his heavy frown. 'It's been known to happen.'

'Who? Your father?'

I could have denied it, kept up the years-long pretence. But time was too precious to waste on falsehoods. So I nodded. 'Yes.'

Axios moved towards me, his frown a dark cloud. 'What did he do to you?'

I hesitated now, because on the flipside I didn't want to bare my all to him. The desire to continue living on my own terms hadn't diminished an iota since my return to Greece. And even if I intended to agree to Axios's demands I would always keep one small corner of my life free from his interference.

'He manipulated every relationship I ever had in some way. I don't want that to happen with Andreos.'

The grey gaze boring into mine stated blatantly that he wanted more. Mine declared I'd given him all I intended to.

'I've seen you with Andreos. He thrives under your care. I'd be a fool to jeopardise that.'

Before I could breathe my relief he stepped closer, bringing that bristling magnificence into touching distance. I balled fingers that tingled with the need to feel his vibrant skin under my touch again.

'You have my word I will not interfere. Will you give me yours?'

Again I was mildly stunned that it was a question rather than a declaration. But the searing reminder that giving in to one emotion around Axios was simply the gateway to a flood of other sensations I needed to keep a tight leash on, had me swallowing the desire.

'I will stay for as long as it takes to give you what you need,' I offered.

He accepted it with a simple nod, as if it was nothing to celebrate. And perhaps in the grand scheme of things it wasn't. We were picking up where we'd left off with the added inconvenience of needing to put out more fires than he'd initially anticipated.

After several skin-tingling moments during which he simply stared at me, as if probing beneath my defences to read my secrets, I twisted away, eager to escape those all-seeing eyes.

'I need to get back to Andreos.'

'We're not quite done, Calypso.'

About to ask what else we needed to talk about, I felt my tight throat close even further when he stepped closer. His scent curled around me, reminding me of what had happened on the sofa a short while ago. Had things really got out of hand so quickly? My body still hummed with unspent energy, and my heart hadn't quite settled into its steady cadence.

'I'll come with you to visit my son.'

The throb of possessiveness in his voice sent my senses flaring wide with warning. What exactly that warning was refused to surface as we left his suite.

As it turned out it wasn't necessary to return to the ground floor. Sophia was carefully navigating the stairs, with a sleepy Andreos in her arms. We followed her as she entered the opposite wing of the villa, where a nursery had been set up by a team of designers on the first day of my return.

Seeing us, she smiled. 'We played for a while, but I think he's ready for his nap, *kyria*,' she said softly.

The sight of Andreos fighting a losing battle to stay awake drew a smile from my heart. Handing him over to Sophia even for such a short while had made my heart ache. I knew it would be a million times worse when I had to leave, but somehow I trusted Axios with his care. Sophia's clear devotion to him was an added bonus.

I reached out for him but Axios stepped forward.

'Do you mind?' The demand was gruff but gentle.

In stunned surprise I nodded. Still smiling,

Sophia handed son over to father and discreetly melted away.

The sight of Axios holding his son for the first time shouldn't have brought a thick lump to my throat. The sight of his strong, powerful arms carefully cradling my baby, his throat moving in a convulsive swallow, shouldn't have fired a soul-deep yearning through my body. A yearning for things to be different. For fate not to be so cruel.

Why? Did I wish for things to be different between Axios and I?

Absolutely not.

As for other yearnings—hadn't I already been granted more than enough? I'd prayed for a healthy son and been given the child of my heart. I'd prayed for a little more time and had enjoyed almost four beautiful months.

But the thought of leaving him, even to fight for my health—

'What's wrong?'

I jumped, my gaze rising to see Axios watching me.

'Am I holding him wrong?'

The touch of uncertainty in his voice caught a warm spot inside me and loosened another smile from me as I approached, unable to stop myself from reaching out, kissing Andreos's forehead and cheek, breathing in his sweet and innocent scent.

'No, you're not doing anything wrong.'

Grey eyes so very similar to his son's dropped to the now sleeping Andreos, and his chest slowly expanded in a long breath before he headed over to the brand-new, state-of-the-art cot set out for our baby.

With the utmost care he transferred Andreos from his arms to the cot, barely eliciting any protest from him. Arms thrown up beside his head in angelic abandon, Andreos slept on as his father draped a soft cotton blanket over him, drew a gentle finger down his cheek and straightened.

Still smiling, I glanced over at Axios—and my heart leapt into my throat. Gone was the gentle look he'd bestowed on his son. In its place was a bleak visage full of loss and yearning that made me gasp. Made that pulse of guilt rise again.

The sound drew his attention to me. When he took hold of my arm and steered me out of earshot I tried to think past the naked tingles his touch brought. To think how I could contain the relentless waves of turbulent emotion bent on consuming us.

'I'd like answers to a few questions, Calypso. If you feel so inclined?' he rasped.

Seeing no way to avoid it without collapsing the agreement I'd struck, I nodded.

His hand dropped to my wrist. 'We'll discuss this further over lunch.'

Lunch was an extensive selection of *meze* fit for a small banquet—not the intimate setting for two laid out on one of the three sun-splashed terraces.

Axios must have spotted my surprise as he pulled out my chair because he shrugged. 'I didn't know your preferences so I instructed the chef to prepare a large selection.'

'Oh…thank you.'

His gaze rested on me as he lowered himself into his own chair. 'Again, you sound surprised. Believe it or not I want things to go as smoothly as possible for both of us.'

The knowledge that this included simple things such as what I ate widened the warm pool swelling inside me. Even cautioning myself that it was foolish to entertain such a sensation didn't do anything to stem it as I helped myself to pitta bread and tzatziki, feta cheese and chickpea salad and succulent vine leaves stuffed with lamb and cucumber.

'Where was Andreos born?'

His deep voice throbbed with one simple emotion—a hunger to know. And for the very first time since my decision to live life on my terms, twelve long months ago, I experienced a deep stirring of guilt.

But along with that came a timely warning not to divulge everything. Knowledge was power to men like Axios. Men like my father. And every precious uninterrupted moment with my son was as vital to me as the breath in my lungs.

Although in the past four days since my return, Axios had seemed a little more…malleable. While the man who'd laid down the law and walked away from me in Agistros still lurked in there somewhere, this Axios tended to ask more and command less.

But still I carefully selected the bits of information that wouldn't connect too many dots for him and replied, 'He was born in a small clinic in Kenya, where I was volunteering. He came a week early, but there were no complications and the birth was relatively easy.'

He didn't answer. Not immediately. The glass of red wine he was drinking with his meal remained cradled in his hand and his expression reflective and almost…yearning as he stared into the middle distance.

'I would've liked to be there,' he rasped. 'Very much.'

The warm pool inside me grew hotter, turning

into a jet of feeling spiralling high with emotions I needed to wrestle under control before they got out of hand.

But even as the warning hit hard I was opening my mouth, uttering words I shouldn't. 'One of the nurses filmed the birth…if you'd like to see it?'

What are you doing sharing your most precious moments with him?

He's Andreos's father.

Axios inhaled sharply, the glass discarded as he stared fiercely at me. 'You have a video?'

I jerked out a nod. 'Yes. Would you—?'

'Yes.' The word was bullet-sharp, and the cadence of his breathing altered as his gaze bored into me. 'Yes. Very much,' he repeated.

For the longest time we remained frozen, our gazes locked in a silent exchange I didn't want to examine or define. Soon it morphed into something else. Something equally intimate. Twice as dangerous.

Perhaps it was in the molten depths of his eyes, or in the not so secret wish to relive what had happened upstairs ramping up that ever-present chemistry. Whatever it was, we'd brought it alive on that sofa and now it sat between us, a writhing wire ready to sizzle and electrify and burn at the smallest hint of weakening.

Forcing my brain back on track didn't help. Hadn't we been discussing childbirth? The product of what had happened in a bedroom the last time we were both present in one.

'I'll let you have the recording after lunch,' I blurted, then picked up my water glass and drank simply to distract myself.

From the corner of my eye I watched him lounge back in his seat, although his body still held that coil of tension that never dissipated.

After a moment he picked up his glass and drained it. *'Efkharisto,'* he murmured. 'Now, on to other things. Arrangements are being made to equip you with a new wardrobe. My mother tells me the things you left behind are hopelessly out of date.'

I frowned, the change of subject from the soul-stirring miracle of Andreos's birth to the mundanity of high fashion throwing me for a few seconds. 'I don't need a new wardrobe.'

'Perhaps not—but might I suggest you let the stylists come anyway? Who knows? You might find something you like for our first engagement on Saturday,' he replied.

The last tendrils of yearning had left his voice, to be replaced by the cadence I knew best. One of powerful mogul. Master of all he surveyed. Despite the pleasant heat of the sun a cool breeze whispered over my skin, bringing me harshly back to earth.

'What's happening on Saturday?'

'It's been four days since you returned. It's time we presented you properly to the world. My mother has organised a party in your honour. She was unwell when we married last year, and couldn't make it to the ceremony. She's anxious to meet you. And, of course, she's yet to meet her grandson. Call this a belated welcome, if you will, but several business acquaintances will be there, so it's imperative that everything goes smoothly.'

'Is it really necessary to parade me before your friends and family?'

'I think it's best to put the rumours to rest once and for all. Then we can concentrate on our son.'

While his attention to Andreos warmed my heart, the prospect of being paraded before his family and business didn't. 'And how do you propose we do that? Is there a storyline I need to follow, chapter and verse?'

He smiled as if the thought of playing out a role so publicly was water off his back. 'Leave that to me,' he stated cryptically. 'All I require from you is to present a picture-perfect image of loving wife and mother. I trust I can count on you to do that?'

For the sake of uninterrupted bonding with my son I would go to hell and back. 'Yes.'

Perhaps my agreement was too quick. Perhaps the depth of feeling behind it was too revealing. Whatever, his gaze grew contemplative, stayed fixed on me.

And when he walked away, moments after the meal was done, I got the distinct feeling there were more bumps and curves on this peculiar road I'd taken than I'd initially realised.

CHAPTER SIX

A PRE-PARTY FAMILY MIXER.

A harmless-sounding statement until you were confronted by the full might of the formidable Xenakis clan.

The gathering had been deceptive. Over the course of two hours they'd trickled in—some by car, others by boat. And Axios's formidable-looking brother Neo, looking a little distracted and a lot harassed, had come by sleek helicopter, with the iconic Xenakis Aeronautics logo emblazoned on its side.

Inexorably the trickle became a stream, and then a torrent. By four p.m. the largest salon in the villa, the surrounding terrace and the perfectly manicured lawn were overflowing with aunts, uncles, cousins and distant offshoots—some from as far afield as Australia and New Zealand.

Fascinatingly, despite the low buzz of tension surrounding their interactions, there were no overt signs of dissent.

Perhaps because I was their main focus.

I didn't want to admit it, but the six-hour makeover session I'd endured earlier in the day boosted my confidence now, as impeccably dressed men and couture-clad women approached the place where I stood next to Axios, with a wide-eyed Andreos nestled in my arms.

My hair had been brought back to shoulder-length, layered and trimmed into loose stylish waves that gleamed with new vitality. And the rails upon rails of new clothes hanging in the closets of my vast dressing room, complete with matching accessories and priceless jewellery, were the *pièce de résistance*.

After months of wearing flats and tie-dye sundresses, and ponytailing my hair, the transformation took a little getting used to. While the teardrop diamond necklace glittering just as bright as the pristine white linen shift dress and tan platform shoes were making me feel intensely aware of the kind of circles I'd married into.

The most striking of the women within those intimidating circles was Electra Xenakis—Axios's mother.

Her hair was a distinctive grey, which had been used to enhance her beauty rather than been dyed away, and it framed an angular face, highlighting superb cheekbones and the striking grey eyes she'd passed on to her sons. Tall and slender, with a ramrod-straight posture, she was formidable—until she gave a rare smile. Then warmth radiated from her every pore, and the icy grey palazzo pants and matching top she wore were suddenly not so severe.

On meeting Andreos she dissolved into hearty tears. And that unfettered display of love for her grandchild thawed the cold knot of apprehension inside me, easing my anguish at the thought of a permanent separation from my child.

The distance I'd needed to get my composure back after handing Andreos over to his grandmother lasted mere minutes before I sensed a presence beside me. It wasn't as visceral and all-encompassing as Axios's, but it demanded attention nevertheless.

I glanced up to find Neo Xenakis standing before me.

'I never quite got the chance to welcome you into the family last year.' His tone was measured, his eyes just as probing as his brother's.

'I guess the circumstances weren't exactly… conducive,' I replied.

'*Ochi*, they weren't. But your disappearing act didn't help matters, I expect?'

I stiffened. 'I had my reasons,' I replied.

Without answering, he dropped his gaze to the contents of the crystal tumbler he clutched.

'Whatever they were, I hope it was worth keeping a father from his child?'

Again his tone was more appraising than censorious, as if he was attempting to understand my motives. Again my guilt resurfaced. And this time brushing it away wasn't easy.

Before I could formulate a response, a deeper and more visceral voice asked, 'Is everything all right?'

For me not to have sensed his arrival spoke volumes of the kind of magnetism the Xenakis men possessed. And now Axios had arrived next to me the force of their presence had doubled. Their sole focus was on me, but one set of grey eyes was vastly more potent than the other, sending my composure into free fall.

I took a long, steadying breath to reply, 'We're fine.'

Axios's gaze slid from mine to his brother, a clear question in his eyes.

Neo's expression clouded for a moment, then he shrugged. 'Like your wife said, we're fine. No need to go Neanderthal on me.'

Before either of us could enquire what he meant, he excused himself and struck out for the large gazebo on the south side of the garden, currently decked out with fairy lights and free of guests.

'Is he okay?' I felt compelled to ask.

Axios's gaze stayed on him long enough to see his brother lift a phone to his ear before he turned to me. 'His issues aren't mine to disclose, but Neo is touchy on the subject of babies. Like the rest of the family, news about his nephew's existence surprised him. But, since Andreos is single-handedly winning everyone over, I suspect the circumstances of his arrival will be forgiven soon.'

Had he deliberately excluded himself from that statement? Unwilling for him to see the bite of anguish that distinction brought, I turned my gaze to where the majority of the Xenakis clan had now gathered, choosing to see the bright side.

Andreos was indeed holding centre stage, tucked into his favourite blanket and nestled lovingly within his grandmother's arms. The absolute devotion on the older woman's face eased my heartache, but in the next moment the sudden thought that my own mother hadn't met my son hit me with tornado-strength force.

'What is it?' Axios asked, the eyes that hadn't left my face since his brother's disappearance narrowing.

The fleeting thought to shrug off his question came and went, and I couldn't help the small shaft of pain that came with it. 'My parents haven't met him yet.'

His face tightened, the mention of Yiannis Petras drawing a reaction I would have preferred to leave out of the already fraught atmosphere. I held my breath, ready to fight my corner.

'We can arrange a visit for your mother later... if you wish?'

Surprised by that response, I blinked. 'I do. Thank you.'

After another minute of assessing scrutiny he nodded. 'Whatever your reasons for fleeing Agistros, I accept that I could've handled our last meeting a little better,' he said, his voice a deep rasp.

My lips were parted in shock when another wave of Xenakises wandered over. Axios's droll look and almost-smile told me he'd seen my shock at his apology.

I managed to get my emotions under control beneath his family's probing glances, watching their silent musing as to what had transpired with Axios's stray wife. I was grateful for their circumspection because, as baptisms of fire went, it could have been worse.

It was with far more trepidation that I contemplated my extensive closet three hours after everyone had disappeared into their various guest rooms and private homes to get ready for the main event. The knock on the door barely snagged my attention. Absent-mindedly I responded, my fingers toying with the tie of my bathrobe as I contemplated the stunning array of clothes.

'As much as you seem to enjoy simply staring at them, you do actually have to pick an outfit to wear for the party, you know?' Ax drawled, his deep tone more amused than I'd ever heard him.

I jumped and turned around, barely able to hold back a gasp at the sight of him, standing a few feet away, wearing half of a bespoke tuxedo. His pristine snow-white shirt was half buttoned, but neatly tucked into his tailored trousers, and his bowtie was strung around his neck.

The intimate knowledge of what resided beneath his clothes dried my mouth as I stared, slack-jawed, several superlatives crowding my brain.

Debonair. Breathtaking. Insanely gorgeous.

Slowly the silence thickened and he raised one sleek eyebrow. 'Can I help with anything?'

The hand I waved over my shoulder at the closet was irritatingly fluttery. 'I can't decide what to wear. Meeting your family was one thing... This is a different ballgame.'

His gaze travelled from the top of my hair,

which still held its earlier style, thanks to the expertise of the stylist, then lingered at the belt holding my robe closed, before moving to my bare feet. Each spot his eyes touched triggered fiery awareness.

'You handled my family admirably and won them over with Andreos. Even Neo—and he's a handful at the best of times,' he added dryly. 'You'll excel just as well tonight.'

The deeply spoken reassurance made my heart lurch. To hide its effect I scrambled for something else to concentrate on, and spotted his dangling sleeves and the cufflinks in his hand.

'Do you need help with those?' I asked, even though assisting him would involve stepping closer, breathing in the intoxicating scent that clung to him and never failed to send my senses haywire.

He held out his arms. 'If you wouldn't mind?'

Breath held, in the hope that it would mitigate the erotic chaos stirring to life inside me, I reached for the two halves of his shirtsleeve in one hand and held out the other for the cufflinks. The tips of his fingers brushed my palm as he handed them over, and every inch of my skin responded as if set alight.

Intensely aware that my nipples were hardening, and that a pulse had started throbbing between my thighs, I hurried to finish my task, my own fingers brushing the inside of his wrist in the process.

Axios inhaled sharply, an incoherent sound rumbling from his chest.

Could we not even exchange a common courtesy without feeling as if the world was about to burst into flames?

Evidently not.

Which was probably all the warning I needed to keep my distance. Never to repeat what had happened on his sofa.

'*Efkharisto,*' he murmured, his voice deep and thick.

His eyes were molten, as heated as that needy place between my legs. Unable to withstand his gaze, for fear I'd give myself away, I turned to face the rack of clothes. Of course my senses leaped high when he stepped next to me, then took another step closer to the open closet.

To my shaky memory this was perhaps the first time I'd been this close without having his laser eyes on me. The opportunity to give in to the urge to stare was too hard to resist.

The breadth and packed strength of his shoulders.

The vibrancy of his lustrous hair.

The sharp, mouthwatering angle of his freshly shaved jaw.

Too busy fighting the way every inch of Axios triggered this unwanted but unstoppable reaction, I didn't notice he'd made a selection until he pivoted, the momentary gaping of his shirt delivering one final punch of his sheer magnetism before he drawled, 'You'll look beautiful in any one of these gowns. But this one will do, I think.'

Heat engulfed my face as I reached out and snatched the gown from his hand, hastily stepping back. 'I…thanks.'

'You need help with the zip?' he asked, in a voice thicker than before.

Aware of the dangerous waters I was treading, I shook my head. 'I think I'll manage. Thanks.'

He hesitated for a stomach-churning moment, then nodded. 'I'll return in fifteen minutes. We will go downstairs together, if you wish.'

I nodded my thanks.

Contrary to his stealthy arrival, I was conscious of Ax's departure for the simple reason that he seemed to take the very air out of the room with him, leaving me breathless as I shrugged off the robe and slipped the gown over my head.

Barely paying attention to the design, I zipped it up and stepped into the heels that had been helpfully paired with the dress, spritzed perfume on my neck and wrists, and was adding the finishing touches to my make-up when his knock came.

Very much aware of the silk clinging to my hips and breasts, I prayed my body wouldn't give me away as I opened the door.

For the longest time he simply stared at me. 'Beautiful,' he finally stated, and the sizzling gleam in his eyes only lent him a more dangerous air, rendering all my efforts for composure useless as I accepted there was no level this man couldn't reach in the drop-dead gorgeous stakes.

'Thank you,' I replied, my voice a husky mess.

He held out his arm. I took it, and was still in a semi-daze when we exited the limo at the entrance to the six-star luxury hotel in the middle of Athens where the party was being held.

The moment Ax and I stepped into the ballroom silence fell over the guests, every eye fixed on me.

'I don't know whether to smile or scowl. What's *de rigueur* these days?' I murmured.

'Just ignore them. That's what I do when I feel out of place.'

I laughed, mostly to hide his unabated effect on me. Besides, I couldn't help it, because picturing Axios as a fish out of water was like attempting to imagine what the landscape inside a black hole looked like.

'Something funny?'

'You wouldn't look out of place amongst a clutch of nuns in a prayer circle.'

He smiled, and just like that my body went into free fall, breaking one tension while ratcheting up another. And as I was crashing down, towards some unknown destination, it struck me that this was the first time I'd seen any semblance of a smile from the man I called my husband.

'An unusual compliment, I think, but thank you all the same,' he said.

'You should've told me the whole of Athens would be here tonight,' I said, a little desperate to maintain a disgruntled distance from him.

He lowered his head even closer to murmur in my ear, 'Put your claws away, *pethi mou*. You look much too beautiful to pick a fight.'

'I'm sure we can find something to fight about if we look hard enough.'

Was I really that desperate to start a fight? Simply to stop this unruly attraction in its tracks?

His amusement disappeared, to be replaced with the unwavering regard that never failed to trigger mini-earthquakes inside me. My breath snagged in my throat as he stepped closer, until there was nothing but a whisper of space between us. To anyone observing us we'd look as if we were sharing an intimate moment. But I knew what was coming even before he spoke.

'Keep tossing those little challenges at me, Calypso, and I'll delight in picking you up on one.'

The electric promise in those words sent a bolt through me. It lingered through all the introductions to influential individuals, A-list celebrities and even more of the Xenakis clan and it slowly began to re-energise, that spark of rebellion reignited.

For some reason I *wanted* to challenge him.

So when I found a moment's reprieve I looked up from my untouched glass of champagne into his face. 'Do you know what I think, Axios?'

A simple but effective hitch of his brow commanded me to continue.

'I don't think you will pick me up on any challenge. I don't think you'll do anything to risk this reputation you're bent on protecting.'

'Are you brave enough to test your theory, I wonder?' he asked, and something untamed pulsed beneath his civil exterior. Something that made the glass in my hand tremble wildly.

His gaze dropped to it before returning to my face. With a wicked smile he raised one imperious hand and traced his knuckles down my heated cheek.

'Pick your battles with care, Calypso. You look stunning in this dress—every eye in the room keeps returning to you time and again, and I'm the envy of every man here. You should be celebrating that, not picking a fight with your husband.'

With that, he leaned even closer, replaced his hand with his mouth for the briefest of moments…

And then he walked off.

Leaving me shaking with a cascade of emotions.

The only reason I felt out of sorts was because that little incident in my dressing room had thrown me—shown me a different side to Axios that had intensified the illicit yearning inside me. And while standing next to Axios wreaked havoc with my equilibrium, watching him, the most prominent man in the room, walking away left me with a yawing hollow in the pit of my stomach.

Did I really want him? Or was I just terrified by the knowledge that the only eyes I wanted on me were his, not the guests' who kept coming up to me, some blatantly questioning why the great Axios Xenakis had tied himself down to *me*.

I shook my head, hoping to clear it of these confusing thoughts.

'I hope you're not shaking your head because you wish to deny me your company?'

I attempted to control my bewildering thoughts before turning towards another one of Ax's cousins.

At my blank look he said, 'I'm Stavros. We met earlier.'

I nodded, attempted to smile. 'Hello.'

His smile was reserved, but genuine. I found myself wishing for another smile. One that was edged in sizzling grey. I was really losing it.

'Having fun?'

I shrugged. 'I'm in a room full of some of the most powerful people on earth, sipping champagne and enjoying the status of hostess with the mostest. What's not to love?'

As with most of the Xenakis clan, his expression grew speculative. 'You sound…distressed. Is everything all right?'

About to answer, I looked across the room to where Ax had been talking to the trade minister moments ago. He was staring directly at me, as if he could see to the heart of my jumbled emotions.

That he could do that from across the room panicked me and irked me. Nevertheless, I had to hold on to what was important. And that was Andreos. Regardless of my personal situation,

I couldn't afford for anything to jeopardise my time with my child.

With a deep breath, I forced a smile and turned to Stavros. 'I'm absolutely fine, Stavros. Sorry if I sounded a little off. Chalk it up to missing my baby.'

'Ah, a little separation anxiety, *ne*? As the father of young children, I remember that state well, too.'

'Yes… Speaking of which, would you mind excusing me? I'd like to call and check on him.'

This time Stavros's smile was a little tight. 'Of course. But I hope you'll honour me with a dance when you return?'

For some reason his request made me glance at Ax. He was once again engrossed in conversation with a clutch of men who were no doubt hanging on his every word.

That spark of rebellion returned and I answered Stavros's smile. 'Maybe. We'll see…'

Excusing myself, I wove through the crowd, my pinned-on smile beginning to fray a little more at the edges every time I was stopped by a well-meaning guest wishing to very *belatedly* congratulate me on my marriage and Andreos's birth, while subtly probing for cracks in my demeanour.

True to his word, Axios had taken care of all

the speculation and chosen the most direct explanation for my absence.

'My wife wished to have a peaceful pregnancy and took the time she needed to safely deliver our son.'

Only the most daring would choose to probe my absence after that.

All evening I'd watched him hold court, effortlessly exuding power and charm over hardcore businessmen and moguls I'd only read about in the newspapers.

And while the wedding last year and the family gathering earlier had already shown me his authority and charisma, watching him speak to and mingle with some of the most influential people in the world truly rammed home to me the almost frightening power he wielded.

He was a powerful man whom my father had managed to bend to his will. A man whose reputation I'd put in jeopardy with my disappearing act.

Had I been fooling myself by striking a deal with him?

Enough! Running rings around my decisions was futile.

I stepped out onto the thankfully empty terrace of the grand hotel ballroom and called Sophia. Reassured that all was well, my thoughts flew as they often did when I thought of Andreos to the battle that awaited me. To the fear that my time with him would be cut short.

My hand dropped to linger over my stomach, to the dull ache residing deep inside…

'Are you all right?' Axios demanded with a gravel-rough voice.

I jumped and whirled around, hastily dropping my hand when his gaze moved to it. 'You're spying on me now?'

He sauntered towards me. 'I came to check on you because I didn't want you to feel neglected. And I haven't forgotten that you fled your marriage after one day and didn't return for a year,' he returned with sizzling fire.

'Because you were happy to leave me alone on your island without a care for what *I* wanted. Have you forgotten that? Did it even occur to you that I might want a different life for myself other than what *you* chose for me?'

For the longest time he didn't reply. Then, 'That was an error in judgement. One I regret,' he intoned solemnly.

The unequivocal apology had the same effect as the one earlier. My jaw dropped. 'You…do?'

'*Ne*,' he drawled.

For another charged moment he stared at me. Then his gaze dropped to my phone.

Almost dazedly I stared at it. 'You can stand down your spies. I was simply calling Sophia to check on my son.'

A deeply possessive look glinted in his eyes. 'He's *our* son, *pethi mou*. Yours and mine and no one else's.'

The very idea of Andreos being anyone else's child but Axios's was so profoundly impossible I almost laughed out loud. And then that notion faded under the weight of the electrified atmosphere crackling between us. The feeling of being caught on the edge of a lightning storm that never quite went away.

It didn't take a genius to see that Axios was in an equally edgy mood.

Attempting to dissipate it, I waved the phone at him. 'He's fine, by the way. According to Sophia, he went down without a fuss.'

Axios shrugged. 'He's almost four months old. I believe that as long as he's warm and well fed he has very little to worry about.'

'It's a little more complicated than that. He needs love and laughter. He's also at the stage where he'll really start recognising his mother's absence.'

Bleakness flashed across his face, momentarily slashing my insides. 'What about his father's? And whose fault is it that I'm not fully equipped with that information, Calypso?' His voice throbbed with raw emotion.

'Axios—'

His hand slashed through the air a split-second before he closed the gap between us and settled his hands on my shoulders. 'I want to move on from this. But there are questions you still haven't answered.'

My heart dipped. 'Like what?'

'What's the big secret about your whereabouts? I hunted for you high and low. My investigators visited Nicrete—discreetly, of course, since I had to protect my family from untoward gossip. The general consensus there was that Calypso Petras was far too level-headed, far too considerate to have made such a selfish move. At least without assistance or coercion of some sort. Perhaps from a source no one had considered.'

'What source?'

His tension heightened, his whole body seemingly caught in a live electric feed. 'You tell me.'

'Maybe a secret admirer? Perhaps even another man?' I taunted.

A fierce little muscle ticked in his jaw. 'Was it? Considering you were a virgin, I wasn't inclined to think you would jump into another man's bed that easily. Tell me I wasn't wrong,' he bit out.

He hadn't thought the worst of me.

The idea of it left me nonplussed for several seconds, considering he still had no idea of my whereabouts for the past year. Considering he had to have overheard some of the blatant whispers at the party.

'Why the interrogation? I thought you were all about keeping up appearances? Convincing the world that my absence was a well-orchestrated plan?'

'That's been taken care of. The results will be evident soon enough. Let's discuss us,' he said, then immediately frowned as if he hadn't expected to say that.

Perhaps he hadn't. After all, wasn't he the man who'd never engaged in a relationship that lasted more than a few weeks?

'*Us?* Are you sure? You seem as surprised by that word falling from your lips as I am to hear it.'

For the longest time he stared at me. Then he shrugged. 'Only a fool stays on a course that's doomed. Perhaps I'm embracing new changes. Attempting to be…different.'

My heart lurched, even as I tamped down fruitless hope. All this meant nothing. Not if my prognosis was as dire as my senses screamed that they were. Not if this marriage was ticking down to dissolution.

'Can we not do this here? I'd like to go back in.'

'Why? So Stavros can succeed at working his angle?'

I blinked in surprise. 'What are you talking about?'

He edged me back a step, following me so we were wedged against the stone balustrade. 'Just a heads-up. His marriage is on the rocks. He's attempting to raise his stature by undermining my authority every chance he gets— chances which, unfortunately for him, haven't been readily available. I'd rather not see you be his pawn,' he breathed, his voice absolutely lethal while being so soft.

Too late, I accepted that the fire inside me was building out of control. His body surged closer, reminding me in vivid detail of the hard-packed, streamlined definition of muscle beneath his bespoke suit. And the fact that his body could render me speechless with very little effort.

'You can stand down. I can take care of myself.'

'*Ne*, I'm beginning to see that,' he murmured, and again there was the barest hint of grudging acceptance in his eyes.

But I didn't get the chance to explore the discovery because his head slowly lowered.

Hot, sensual and commanding, his lips slanted

over mine. With a gasp that was way too husky
and way too revealing I threw up my hands.
Somewhere in the back of my head I was aware
that I'd dropped my phone. But it didn't seem to
matter, because his tongue was delving between
my lips, seeking entrance I was helpless to deny.

He tasted me with a brazenness that struck a
match to the desire that had been straining to be
freed after that episode on his sofa. With effort-
less ease he set it ablaze between one snatched
breath and the next.

His tongue stroked mine with a possessiveness
that took control of my whole body, so that when
one hand slid from my shoulder and down my
back to draw me into sizzling contact it felt as
if I was made of warm, pliant dough, ready to
mould myself to any shape of his bidding.

When his other hand angled my head to deepen
the kiss it was all I could do to slide my own
hands around his neck. To hold on tightly as the
dizzying journey zipped like a rollercoaster ride
I never wanted to end.

With a helpless moan, I parted my lips wider,
strained onto my toes the better to absorb more
of the experience.

Ax made a gruff sound that disintegrated beneath our frenzied kiss. His hold intensified until
we were plastered together from chest to thigh.

Until the unmistakable imprint of his thick, aroused manhood blazed hot and potent against my belly.

My fingers convulsed in his hair as the memory of him inside me, possessing me, surged into life. Feverish need pooled between my thighs, hunger prising another moan from my throat.

Before it could be anywhere near sated Ax was pulling away, his gaze searingly possessive as it moved from my damp and tingling mouth to my eyes.

'Now that we've shown the world how hot we still are for each other, will you come inside with me and dance with your husband?' he asked, his tone husky but firm.

Did he really want to dance with me or had he kissed me just for show?

The eyes burning into mine seemed to be attempting to read me just as hard as I was trying to reading him.

What was he looking for?

What was *I* looking for?

My scrambling senses flailed, and I was aghast at how easily and completely he'd overtaken my senses. How even now, with a few snatched breaths, I still couldn't think beyond the need to experience that kiss all over again. Yearning for more than just a kiss.

Realising he was awaiting a response, I scrambled the appropriate words together. 'Yes. If I must.'

He swooped down to pick up my discarded phone, then linked his fingers with mine before tugging me after him.

The crowd parted at our re-entrance, and some of the gazes I met were alight with the knowledge of what we'd been doing out on the balcony.

Being mired in my confused emotions saved me feeling embarrassment at those looks. It also made me pliant enough to survive half of the slow waltz with Axios before my senses began to return.

The reality of finding myself plastered to my husband once more, with the effects of that kiss still lingering in the form of my peaked nipples and erratic breathing, made me glance wildly around, avoiding his gaze as I tried to gather my shredded composure.

'Look at me, Calypso,' he instructed gruffly.

Almost helplessly I met his gaze.

His expression was studiously neutral but his eyes glinted with residual emotion. 'What just happened is nothing to be ashamed of,' he said gruffly. 'In fact, some might think it…fortunate that we're compatible in some ways.'

I wanted to laugh, because he was oh, so savvy about such things. While I continued to flounder.

'Don't you think it's a touch…*needy* to feel you have to be the centre of everyone's attention?' I asked.

The arrogant smile he slanted down at me said he didn't care one way or the other what people thought.

'I don't wish to be the centre of everyone's attention. Just yours,' he drawled.

For the sake of our audience, I sternly reminded myself, even as my insides lurched and jumped with misguided giddiness.

To mitigate that sensation I pressed my lips together and swayed in his arms, hoping the music would soothe my ragged nerves and spirit the rest of this infernal night away.

But, as fate had shown me time and again, hopes and dreams belonged in fairy tales. Axios danced me through three more tunes before conceding the fourth to the mayor.

Thereafter, quickly reclaimed by my so-called doting husband, we moved from group to group, his hand firm on my waist and his piercing grey eyes smiling down at me through each introduction.

His acting skills were exceptional. Our guests

lapped up every soft caress, indulgently smiling at my every recounting of why I'd been away as if it was a true Greek love story.

We stopped within every circle long enough to project an image of cordiality before moving on. And I regurgitated the practised story of my absence until I feared I was blue in the face. Until I was ready to scream the truth to the whole world.

Perhaps his shark-like instincts sensed my frazzling composure. Because Ax turned to me as I impatiently waved away another offer of champagne and started to open my clutch.

'What is it?' he asked.

Remembering he had possession of my phone, I looked at him. 'Can I have my phone back? I want to check on Andreos.'

His gaze rested on my face for several beats. Thinking he wasn't going to answer, I was surprised when he turned to the business acquaintances he'd been talking to.

'It's time for us to take our leave. My beloved cannot bear to be away from our son for long, and I find that I'm not far behind her in that sentiment.'

Indulgent laughter followed, quick goodbyes were said, and before I knew it we were heading out to the waiting limo.

Settled into the back seat, I found my senses once again crowded with the sight and sound of Axios. My inability to dismiss him.

'I could've gone home on my own. You didn't need to leave with me.'

One sleek eyebrow spiked. 'You wanted me to stay there and reverse the effect of everything we've achieved this evening?' he replied.

'You seem to be a master at convincing everyone that the moon is made of caviar. I'm sure they'll believe whatever you tell them.'

He gave a low, deep laugh. Which drained away as his eyes latched to my face. 'Perhaps I do have this unique gift you speak of, but I also meant what I said. I've missed months of my son's life. I don't intend to miss any more.'

'For how long?'

His whole body froze. 'Excuse me?'

'How long do you think this phase of yours will last?'

'You have lost me...'

A thought that had been niggling me despite his assertion rose to the fore. 'You didn't want this marriage and we never got around to discussing children. We're only here because a condom failed at the crucial juncture.'

'And you think those circumstances beyond

my control preclude me from assuming my mantle of responsibility towards my son? Did it you?'

'I… It's different.'

'How?' he challenged.

'I love him! I would do anything for him. While you…'

'What? Speak your mind, *glikia mou.*'

'You just want to show off your virility.'

After several tense seconds he settled back in his seat. 'You're right. I do want to show him off. He is my son, after all. As for showing off my virility—again, the evidence is there for all to see. But, while you're wrong if you think you're the only one invested in Andreos's existence, I'm aware that only time will prove what I say to you. So I guess the ball's in your court on that one.'

'How so?'

'You're the one who's in a hurry to leave. You say you were always going to come back? I'm choosing to believe you. If you want to ensure my devotion to my son is as strong as yours, then you need to rethink the urgency of your divorce demands, do you not, *pethi mou*?'

Despite his silky tone his eyes bored into mine in the dark interior of the car, and the notion that he was attempting to see right into my soul assailed me.

The thick lump wedged in my throat stalled my answer. Because *time* was the one commodity I might not have.

CHAPTER SEVEN

THE LIMO SWEEPING through the gates of his Athens mansion drew from me a breath of relief. But I soon realised I wasn't going to be set free from Ax's presence when he trailed me up the stairs to the door of Andreos's room.

I hesitated before the doors—partly because I didn't want to bring charged tension into Andreos's presence and partly because a tiny part of me wanted space to dissect everything that had happened this evening. But the greater part of me wanted to keep my son all to myself. Just for a little while.

A sharp cry from within dissipated every thought.

As Ax held the door open for me I entered the room in time to see Sophia lifting Andreos from his changing mat.

She stopped and smiled when she saw us. 'Good evening, Kyria Xenakis. You're just in time for Andreos's midnight feed. Would you like me to warm the bottle for you?'

I waved her away and Ax strode forward to

take Andreos from her arms. 'Go to bed, Sophia. I'll take care of it.'

With a smiling nod, the young girl retreated to the adjoining bedroom, shutting the door behind her.

Ax adjusted his hold on Andreos, his strong hands lifting him aloft so they were face to face. My breath caught and, recalling his words in the car, I watched father and son stare at each other, one expression showing unabashed curiosity while the other probed with raw intensity as Axios absorbed his son's every expression as if hoarding it for his memory.

A little ashamed at questioning his motives in the car, I bit my lip as something settled inside me. No matter our personal angst, Axios cared for his son. Perhaps in time he'd love him almost as much as I did.

In that moment I wanted to tell him he would have years of special moments like this if I didn't manage to defuse the time bomb ticking inside me, but the words remained locked tight in my throat, the need not to have this time diluted with unwelcome outside influence stilling my tongue as I joined them.

Sensing another presence, Andreos turned towards me, his chubby arms windmilling as he babbled in delight. Then delight turned into familiar irritation as hunger kicked in and he whimpered his displeasure.

'Someone is impatient for his feed,' Ax mused, before his gaze dropped pointedly to my chest.

A fierce blush suffused my face. My breasts had been growing heavier in the last couple of hours. Even without the need to feed him myself I would have needed to express some milk before going to bed.

Expecting Ax to hand him over, I watched in surprise when he headed to the antique rocking chair I used for feeding Andreos. 'You're staying?'

'Unless you have an objection?' he asked, and I realised it was a genuine query.

About to say yes, I stunned myself by shaking my head.

A look flitted across his face faster than I could decipher it before he nodded. Once I was seated in the chair, which I'd discovered had been in his family for generations, Ax handed Andreos over. Then he started to move towards the adjacent sofa.

'Um…' I said.

He turned immediately. 'What is it?'

'Can you help me with my dress?'

Piercing grey eyes darkened a fraction as they moved to the halter neck of my dress. He gave a brisk nod, and in one deft move freed the fastening.

I caught the front before I was completely exposed, but there was no hiding from Ax's focused attention as I positioned Andreos on my lap.

He latched on with greedy enthusiasm, one fist planted firmly on my breast while both chubby legs jerked up to wrap around the forearm of the hand I'd laid on his plump belly to steady him.

The familiar action tugged at my heartstrings and drew a smile.

'Does he always do that?' Ax rasped, his voice gruff with emotion.

For a precious few seconds I'd forgotten he was there, watching my every move, absorbing his son's routine. Now my gaze met his and I nodded shakily, strangely overcome to be sharing this little snippet of time with the man who'd helped create my precious son.

'Since he was two and a half months old. I think it's his way of telling me to stay put. He'll let me go when he's satisfied.'

Ax lounged back in his seat and crossed his legs, a curious, heart-stopping little smile playing at his sensuous lips. 'He's a Xenakis. He knows what he wants.'

That display of unabashed male pride would

have been unbecoming from any other man. From Ax it was a solid statement acknowledging his progeny. Progeny that would be completely his if I lost my fight.

The lance of pain to my heart made my breath catch.

'What is it?' Ax asked sharply. 'Does it cause you pain?'

My gaze flew to his and I had to swallow before I could answer. 'The breastfeeding? No, it doesn't.'

His narrowed gaze moved from Andreos and back to me. 'Then what is it?'

I flailed internally as I tried to find a plausible response. 'I was just remembering our conversation in the car. Perhaps I was…a little harsh.'

One brow quirked, but it was minus the mockery I'd become used to. *'Perhaps?'*

'Okay, I was. I… I don't want us to butt heads over Andreos.'

His hands spread in a manner that suggested a truce. 'Neither do I, Calypso.'

As milestones went, this was another sizeable one in an evening filled with small earthquakes of surprise. My breath caught. Andreos whimpered. I looked down to find eyes so much his father's wide and curious upon me. Reading my every expression just as intently as his father probed beneath my skin.

'Maybe we should discuss this further later?'

'I agree,' Ax responded, then proceeded to watch me with hawk-like intensity all through the feed.

When I transferred Andreos to my other breast Ax's gaze tracked my blush after dropping once to my nipple. But this time my self-consciousness was reduced. The natural act of providing sustenance for my baby was one I realised I didn't mind sharing with his father.

Just as abruptly as he'd wrapped his sweet limbs around my arm Andreos dropped his legs and he detached with a loud plop.

Ax rose and sauntered over, wordlessly securing my dress as I sat Andreos on my lap and rubbed his back. I was rewarded with a loud burp three minutes later.

With a gentle caress of his son's head, Ax stepped away. 'I have a few phone calls to make. I'll meet you in my suite when you're done here.'

The reminder that our suites were interconnecting and the memory of what had happened in his sent a pulse of electricity through me as I watched him walk away.

His icy indifference had receded. Something had happened on that balcony tonight. The realisation that Ax didn't tar me with the same brush as my father had eased something in me.

I was pondering the new path this might lead to as I laid a sleepy Andreos back in his cot and then entered the suite forty-five minutes later.

Both the living room and bedroom in Ax's suite were empty. Entering my own suite, I crossed to the dressing room, quickly undressed, then slid on my night slip before throwing a matching silk gown over it.

I was brushing my hair at my dressing table when Ax walked in, both hands in his pockets.

He paused in the doorway, his eyes holding a skin-tingling expression and resting on me for a long moment before he prowled forward. He stopped behind me and I waited, my breath locked in my throat as one hand reached out, tugged the brush from me and slowly dragged it through my hair.

For a full minute he said nothing, and the hypnotic sensation of his movements flooded my system with torrid lust.

'You'll be pleased to know our strategy worked,' he drawled eventually. 'My family and friends believe we are happily reunited. I expect my business partners to fall in line by morning.'

Something shook inside me. The easy way he laid his hand on me was a stronger warning that things were shifting. That the conversation on the balcony had indeed sparked much more than a rebellion and the need to answer it in both of us.

Before I could heed the warning he nudged me to my feet, slid his hand down my arm to link with my fingers. 'Come with me.'

Even the imperious tone had altered, become less…autocratic.

I followed him into his living room.

There, on a wide screen, he'd set up the video I'd given him. 'Ax…?'

'I haven't had a chance to watch this yet. Or perhaps I was putting it off,' he said, with a hint of vulnerability in his voice that stunned me enough to take the seat next to him when he settled on the plush sofa.

'You want to watch it now?' I asked.

His eyes met mine, held me in place. 'Yes,' he stated simply.

With a flick of his finger on the remote the video came to life. The simple but clean walls of the hospital room in Kenya came into view before the camera swung over the machines to rest on my heavily pregnant form.

My breath strangled into nothing as the uniquely intimate and life-changing event unfolded on the screen, tugging at the very heart of me.

Beside me Ax caught his breath audibly as he watched a contraction hit me, and the hand that still held mine tightened. This footage had been taken about ten minutes before Andreos's birth. Ax watched every frame without taking his gaze off the screen, his whole body rapt as Andreos was laid in my arms for the first time. He watched me kiss his wrinkled forehead, heard me murmur, 'My little miracle,' as tears of joy spilled down my face.

His throat moved in a swallow when the video ended, and he immediately hit 'rewind' and watched it all over again.

Then his gaze shifted to me.

'Ax...'

He shook his head, raised my hand to his mouth, gently kissed the back of it. 'It was a magnificent birth.'

Deep inside me something *essential* melted, pulling me into a dangerous spell I wasn't entirely certain I wanted to fight. Emotion clogging my throat, I smiled.

'He's a beautiful boy,' he rasped, a throb of deep pride in his voice.

I blinked unbidden tears away. 'Yes. He is.'

'As beautiful as his mother.'

As my breath caught all over again, his thumb rubbed across my knuckles.

'Again you have my thanks—especially since you had to go through that alone.'

'I'd do anything for him,' I replied, and I knew the fervent well of my emotion had registered with him.

For the longest time he simply stared, then his gaze returned to the screen, his vision going a little hazy. 'The reality of him—' He stopped. 'He may be an unexpected arrival in my life, but I want the chance to do right by him. To do things differently—'

Again he stopped, prompting questions I couldn't halt.

'Differently from what? Your father? I noticed your stiff interaction at the wedding, then again at the family mixer, and assumed *I* was to blame.'

He shook his head. 'Our issues go back a little further. I was still a teenager when my grandfather announced that I was to be his successor. In his eyes my father didn't have what it took to make the tougher decisions.' A muscle ticked in his jaw as his lips firmed. 'My father disagreed. He attempted to prove my grandfather wrong.'

I frowned. 'How?'

'My grandfather temporarily handed him the reins of the company. Six months later my father suffered a breakdown brought on by extreme stress. He didn't take the prognosis well.'

'What did he do?'

'He believed my grandfather had humiliated him. And when my grandfather made it known that he'd seen me as his successor all along, my father...didn't take it well. His resentment festered irreparably.' His lips twisted. 'Which, in a nutshell, is the story of my whole family.'

'But you all seem so...*united*—give or take the odd vibe or two.'

He shrugged cynically. 'Self-interest, especially where wealth is concerned, has a way of binding even the most dissenting individuals. My father may not like the status quo but he's had to accept it.'

'Is there no way to repair your relationship?'

A hint of bleakness came and went in his eyes within a heartbeat. 'We've accepted our strengths and our weaknesses. My father may resent me for seemingly usurping him, but he doesn't want the role.'

'You offered it to him?'

His lips thinned. 'A few years ago I suggested a partnership. He refused.'

'He wanted all or nothing?'

His lips twisted. 'Don't we all?'

Pain lashed me. 'Not all of us. Our fathers, maybe.'

Grey eyes met mine and a moment of affinity lingered between us, threatening to burrow into vulnerable places.

I cleared my throat. 'Is that why you're determined to try with Andreos?'

He'd said on the balcony that he was attempting to be different. The part of me that wasn't terrified of what the future held desperately craved to see that difference.

The question took him aback, and a naked yearning blanketed his features before he mastered it. 'Is it wrong to wish for a better outcome with my son than that between my father and I?' he rasped.

Again, a deep, sacred sensation pulled at me. Harder. Stronger. Making it impossible to breathe.

Despite the danger of falling under the silken spell he was weaving, I laid my hand on his arm. 'No, it's not.'

His gaze dropped to my hand. Silence charged with electricity filled the room as something flashed in his eyes. Primal and fierce. The video and our conversation had done something to him. Shifted the dynamic.

I was tempted to run. To hide from it. But I was just as determined not to regress.

'So…where do we go from here? After tonight, I mean?'

His eyes dropped to my lips, then moved back up to seize mine.

'Now we consolidate on what we've started,' he murmured huskily.

I wanted to ask for clarity. Wanted to ask whether he meant us or the larger world. But his fingers wound tighter around mine, his free hand rising to slide into my hair, dragging over my scalp in a wickedly evocative move that snatched the air from my lungs and hardened my nipples into aroused peaks.

Those penetrating eyes tracked my every re-action, his nostrils flaring when he caught the visible signs of my agitated state.

'And how do you propose to do that?' I asked.

'By making things real both inside and out-side of the marriage bed,' he stated, his voice deep and sure.

Lightning-hot excitement charged through me, the need to experience this altered Axios over-whelming me. Would the change he wanted with his son manifest itself with me too, even in the short time I might have?

Only one way to find out.

I tugged myself free and stood to my feet.

Mutiny flashed in his eyes.

When he started to reach for me, I held up a hand. 'If you want me to change my mind convince me that you're worth it,' I said.

Then I fled.

I went after her like a beast possessed.

She was mine.

My wife.

All evening I'd caught tantalising glimpses of her. The way she moved, the thoughtful way she responded to strangers' rabid curiosity, even accommodating Stavros…

I'd run the gamut from telling myself I didn't care about all the facets of herself she was revealing to feeling a determination to pin her down and extract every last secret from her.

But that video…

Her father was in possession of a hundred million euros. My name could have commanded an entire wing in a plush private hospital. And yet Calypso had chosen to deliver our son in a state-run hospital in Kenya with third-rate equipment. And, not only that, she'd done all that with an inner strength that shone through the footage, surrounded by people who had clearly held her in high regard.

She'd spent some of the past year volunteering. I couldn't name a single member of my family who would devote their time to charity unless it came with a tax write-off or a star-studded gala where they could show off their diamonds.

And besides the awe-inspiring act of giving birth, the most striking thing about Calypso Xenakis was the determination I'd seen on her face in that video.

It had sparked something inside me. A need for...*more.*

That intoxicating little incident on the sofa this afternoon, compounded by the kiss on the balcony this evening and watching her nurse our son, was what had finally fully awakened the primitive beast inside me. The video was evidence of her strength and resilience, despite my less than stellar behaviour last year.

Even confessing the true relationship between myself and my father—a subject I'd never discussed with another living soul—had felt... liberating. That we were both products of our circumstances had triggered an affinity in us that had in turn laid out a different way to approach what had been thrust on us.

Perhaps it didn't need to be finite.

That admission to do things differently this time had surprisingly settled deep inside me.

The Calypso I'd married had possessed a banked fire.

The woman who'd returned from her mysterious absence was flame and grit.

Heat I was unashamedly drawn to. Grit I wanted to explore.

Both characteristics drove me after her.

I arrived in the suite just as she was entering her own bedroom. I stopped her with the simple act of capturing her delicate wrist. The electricity of contact simply reaffirmed my decision.

She waited, one eyebrow elevated.

Theos mou, did she know how alluring she was, with her blue eyes daring me even as her agitated breathing announced that she wasn't unaffected by this insane chemistry?

'I want you, Calypso. And unless I'm wildly off-base you want me too.'

'That's it? Surely you have better negotiating skills than that, Axios?' she taunted.

The breathless sound of my name on her lips escalated the heat pounding through my bloodstream. I wanted to kiss her. To prove with deeds instead of words how combustible this thing between us was.

'You're not the same woman I left on Agistros last year. I see that now.'

More than that, she had the power to walk away again if she chose.

The strange sensation of being on slippery ground forced me into further speech, even as I questioned the wisdom of the route I was taking.

'Come to my bed—not because of our agreement or because of your ultimatum. Do it because you want to. Because we can make each other feel things we've never experienced before.'

Her lips parted in a soft gasp. 'You… I do that to you?'

I couldn't help the hoarse laughter that was ejected from my throat. I dropped her wrist and removed myself several mind-clearing paces away.

'Barely two hours ago, I was close to saying to hell with propriety and taking you on that balcony. What do *you* think?'

Despite the heat flaming up her face her shoulders went back, accepting her power over me. It was all I could do to remain standing where I was and not stride across the room to demonstrate just how much the hunger inside me lashed through her too.

But this was too important.

I wasn't an animal, and she needed to grant me clear acknowledgement of her desire before it would work. But it *was* going to work. There were no viable alternatives to allay this…this insane *craving* inside me save for the highly unsatisfactory avenue of self-pleasure, which I wasn't willing to consider any more.

'I'm a man with healthy appetites, Calypso. And I haven't had sex since our wedding night. Do you know that?'

She gave another gasp, this time a heated one that went straight to my groin. She backed against the door, as if putting distance between herself and the live wire of desire lashing us would work.

Eyes wide, she lifted her chin in further challenge. 'How do I know that's true?'

Frustration threatened to erupt. I tamped it down. 'I don't make a habit of lying, *yineka mou*. Regardless of how we came together, I took a vow I intend to honour until I'm no longer bound by it. But if you don't believe me I can give you the number of a top investigator and you can discover the truth for yourself.'

'Even if I believe you, maybe you didn't seek another woman's bed because you didn't want to jeopardise your precious deal.'

She was really good at pushing my buttons. And the curious thing was that I preferred this version of Calypso to the one who'd glided down the aisle a little over a year ago.

I shrugged off my tuxedo, watched her gaze cling to my torso before another blush pinkened her smooth skin. 'Whatever my reason for staying celibate, I wish it to end now.'

'Because you decree it?'

'Because you're woman enough to admit you want me too. Because *when* you come to my bed it'll be because your needs are as strong as mine and you're not ashamed to give in to them.'

Tossing the jacket aside, I gave in to the urge and returned to her, my senses jumping at the promise of decadent friction when she swallowed but stayed her ground. And then, because I wasn't above playing dirty to get my way, I unbuttoned one shirt stud. Then another.

Brazenly, I revelled in the tremor that went through her lush frame as her eyes followed my undressing with abashed appreciation. A layer of femininity which might have been there all along or I might have missed called to the beast in me.

'I want to lay you on my bed…make you cry out my name in climax.'

Her eyelashes fluttered before sweeping down. That tell-tale sign that she was hiding something nearly derailed me. It certainly froze me in place, congealing my insides with the knowledge that, far from being a forward-thinking man, some things were sacred to me.

'Tell me what you're thinking.'

She remained silent for far too long. In real time it was probably a handful of seconds. But it was enough to unnerve me. Enough that when she deigned to lift those hypnotising eyes to mine all that remained in me was a frenzied roar.

I watched her lips move but didn't hear the words she uttered. Her eyes grew wider, possibly at my expression. She started to step back.

I closed the gap between us and tugged her to me. With her heavy magnificent breasts pressed against my chest all I wanted was to lose myself in her. To slay this terrible *need*.

Her nostrils quivered as she inhaled rapidly. Against my chest her hands fluttered, and a trembling I wanted to believe had nothing to do with sex seized her.

'Axios...'

'I said I want to be different, Calypso. Take this leap with me?'

But even as her eyes widened at my words she hesitated, her lower lip caught between her teeth, taunting me with the prospect of unaccustomed denial.

And all the while my insides churned with emotions I didn't want to examine.

All the while delicate tremors filtered through her body and her breathing grew more erratic with her undeniable arousal.

I was on the very edge of my sanity when Calypso's fingers whispered over the button above my navel, toyed with the stud for a second before fluttering away again. Eyes that refused to meet mine remained fixed on my chest.

She released her lip and I fought the urge to lean down and bite the plump, wet curve.

Before her wicked hands could further wreck me, I caught them in one hand. 'Calypso, look at me.'

After an eternity her lashes lifted. Dark blue hypnotic pools pulled me in, threatening to drown me.

'Say the words. I want to hear them,' I pressed, aware that my voice was a gravel-rough mess.

She inhaled. 'I'll take the leap with you. For now.'

I had to hand it to her—she knew how to time her negotiations to maximum effect. But I'd given my word and I wouldn't go back on it. Besides, the earlier we excised this fever from our systems the earlier we could start the extrication process.

The earlier I could return to my life as I knew and preferred it.

The punch of satisfaction I expected never arrived.

More...

'For now?' I repeated, dismissing the hollow echo of the words.

I steeped myself deeper in the moment. Revelled in the fingers gripping my shirt as if the small scrap of cotton would ground her. She swallowed again, then gave a nod.

I crooked a finger under her chin and nudged her head upward. 'Tell me, *pethi mou*,' I insisted.

'I want you,' she whispered.

The breathy little sound washed over my chin and throat, making something frenzied and untamed leap inside me, filling me with the prospect of what 'more' could mean.

'More...' I pressed, wanting irrevocable confirmation that she wanted this.

Her chin lifted, her eyes gleaming boldly. 'I want to be in your bed. I want you to take me.'

I slid my hand up her delicate spine to tangle in her hair. To grip it and keep her attention on me. 'I want to make you mine again. Tell me you want that.'

Her fists bunched, a breathy little sound escaping her throat as she swayed closer. 'I want to be yours.'

Like over a breached dam, a torrent swelled

inside me. Removing her silk dress was as simple as catching the fragile material and ripping it off her body.

She gasped, staring down at the tattered fabric at her feet before attempting to glare at me. 'I don't believe you did that.'

A smile caught me unawares. 'I didn't think you were that attached to it. If so, I'll buy you a dozen more,' I vowed thickly. Because the sight of her body, displaying changes after bearing my son in the form of slightly thicker hips, a rounded softness in her belly and, best of all, the heaviness of her breasts, had intensified the throbbing in my groin.

I was barely aware of sinking to my knees, framing her lush hips and pulling her to me. I welcomed the fingers clenching tight into my hair as my lips found the sensitive flesh below her navel and brazenly tasted her creamy skin. When she sagged against the door I went lower, removing her panties before catching one leg and throwing it over my shoulder so I could find the heart of her, the true feminine core that called to me with the strength of a dozen sirens.

'Ax!'

Her sweet cry urged me on, her taste a drug surging with unstoppable force through my bloodstream. I didn't relent until she was splintering in my arms, her moans music to my ears. Only then did I scoop her up and carry her to my bed to begin all over again.

Her head rolled on the pillow, her hair fanning out in a dark silken halo as her lips parted on hot little gasps as I rediscovered every delightful inch of her body.

'*Omorfi…*'

The word tumbled unbidden from my lips as I caught one pearled nipple in my mouth. And she *was* beautiful, with a certain indefinable layer of femininity and strength adding to her allure.

'When you glided up that aisle like an obedient wraith I had no idea you were hiding this…this steel and sensuality beneath that frothy gown.'

Her eyes widened in dazed surprise. 'Was that why you left the next morning? Because I wasn't what you expected?'

It was my turn to be stunned. To ponder how events had unfolded through her eyes. But now wasn't the time to admit I'd been unnerved then too. Just as I was now.

'No. My delivery wasn't great, but I believed leaving was best. However, *this*…' I slid a hand down her ribcage, revelled in her unfettered response '…was certainly a surprise.'

And the fact that she was even more responsive now threatened to annihilate my self-control completely.

Before I was entirely consumed I reached for a condom, donned it and accepted the enthralling welcome of her parted thighs. I slanted my lips over hers, unwilling to leave any feast unsatisfied as I entered her in one deep, glorifying thrust.

Pleasure detonated in a shower of fireworks as I seated myself deep within her. Felt her tighten around me, drawing me deeper. When she sought to shatter me further with needy whimpers and greedy hands I tore my lips from hers, gritted my teeth in an effort to make this last.

But of course the next layer of sweet torture waited in the wings. With her mouth free, and the nirvana of a higher plane of pleasure waiting, I watched her slide into that unique dimension, that place where her unfiltered pleasure rippled from her alluring lips.

'My God, you're so big. *So* deep. I feel every inch of you…'

A muted roar rumbled up my throat as her words threatened to completely unravel me.

Her nails sank into my back, ripping away another layer of control. And just like on that night I'd never been able to put out of my mind I realised she was unaware of herself, that pleasure had transported her into another dimension.

'Shall I roll my hips like that first time? That was incredible.'

'Calypso...' I wasn't sure whether saying her name was warning or encouragement. Either way, she didn't respond. She continued her mind-altering commentary. Commentary that fired a white-hot blaze inside me alongside the fiery one already raging from possessing her.

I stared down into her stunning, unguarded face as I pushed in and out of her, racing both of us towards that special peak.

Another man would have taken advantage of the situation, prised secrets from her subconscious while she was in this state. But that was an invasion my conscience wouldn't let me stomach for longer than a nanosecond.

So I refocused on the words tumbling from her lips, revelled in them for another reason altogether. Because they turned me on. Because no other woman had brought this unique, exquisite surprise to my bed. Because hearing her vocalise her pleasure charged mine in a way I'd never thought possible.

Increasing the tempo of my thrusts, I lowered my body to hers, drew her tighter against me. 'Wrap your legs around my waist, *omorfia mou*.'

With gratifying speed, she complied.

'Now, tell me more,' I growled in her ear. 'Tell me everything you're feeling.'

Whether she heard me or not, I didn't know, but the words spilled out.

Unmanned by her unfiltered longing, I kissed the corner of her luscious mouth and groaned when she chased mine when I withdrew.

'Kiss me. Please kiss me.'

'Say my name, *matia mou.* Say my name and I'll kiss you.'

'Axios,' she moaned. 'Kiss me, *please*, Axios.'

Unable to resist the sultry demand, I kissed her again. Felt her tighten around me in response and gritted my teeth to keep myself on that dizzying plateau for one more second. She was eroding every ounce of my willpower, pushing me towards the zenith long before I was ready.

And there was little I could do to stop it.

Especially not when my mind was already flying to the next time, to the next position.

She would be on top. Yes, she would ride me, her heavy breasts high and proud, while those unfettered words fell from her lips. The image was so potent, so vivid, I lost the ability to think straight.

My unguarded growl in response to that scenario pushed her higher. Her nails dug into my shoulders, her head thrashing on the pillow.

'Let go, Calypso. Now!'

The command set her free. With a sharp, sweet cry, she dissolved into uncontrollable convulsions, her body writhing beneath mine in innocently uncoordinated movements that finally shattered my control.

With a roar torn from deep within I succumbed to exquisite, untrammelled bliss. Time ceased to matter. I was aware I'd collapsed on top of her, one propped arm the only thing stopping me from crushing her. But her own arms were wrapped tight around me, as if holding me together.

The singular, searing thought that I wanted to remain here *indefinitely* charged through my daze, forcing me to move. Forcing sanity back into this madness.

But even as I gathered her to me after my return from the bathroom she was unravelling me again, the hand on my chest reaching deeper as she turned her face to me.

'Ax?'

'Hmm?' Unfamiliar dread clenched my gut, escalating the notion that somewhere along the line I'd fallen under her mercy and her whim.

Her breath fluttered out in an almost reverent

exhalation as her eyes lifted to mine. 'You're the only man I've ever been with. I just thought you should know.'

That gift, freely given when it could have been withheld in light of our circumstances, punched and winded me. The notion that opening up to her had possibly earned me this unsettled me even more.

Questions and wants and needs surged higher than before, racing to the tip of my tongue before circumspection halted them. I wanted more from her. But did I have more to give to her and to Andreos?

I pushed back the dismaying sensation.

She was staying...for now.

That unsettling little addendum would be tackled later. After much-needed regrouping.

'*Efkharisto.*'

The word emerged deeper, graver than I'd expected. I did nothing to offset it. Nothing but accept that things *had* to be different.

Nothing I'd seen of the marriages around me had fuelled a need to embroil myself in one—not when they strained so easily and threatened to break at the smallest hint of adversity.

But, in the hypothetical scenarios where marriage *had* crossed my mind, I'd known that unshaken faithfulness and stalwart support would be the cornerstone of its success. Not the kind of marriage held together by financial worth—the kind my grandfather had struggled to hold on to and ended up paying dearly for.

That reminder cooled my jets long enough to let in rational thought. Long enough to know that Calypso and I needed a base of trust from which to operate.

Which meant getting her to open up about her secrets...

I decided to come at it from a different angle. 'Are you ready to tell me why you chose to leave Greece?'

Her eyes shadowed and her lashes swept down. But before I could catch her chin and redirect her attention on me she lifted her gaze, her eyes boldly meeting mine with a resolution I wasn't sure whether to welcome or battle.

'Okay.'

Relief stunned me. 'Okay?'

She nodded. 'I want whatever time we have remaining to be peaceful.'

I forced my teeth not to grit at the reminder of a timescale. 'Good.'

A touch of nerves edged her features. When she went to move out of my arms, I caught her back. 'It would please me if you stayed right here for this.'

CHAPTER EIGHT

HE WAS UNRAVELLING ME with his low-voiced requests. With this side of him that hinted at the kind of man I'd dreamed of calling husband and father to my child. The kind of man who asked me to take a leap even when I knew that ultimately my path might lie elsewhere.

Tell him.

Maybe this could all turn out differently.

You could have more nights like this, far into the future.

But what if the worst happened? I couldn't put Andreos through that.

Besides, while Ax had readily agreed to my stipulation…for now…he'd given me no insight as to what would happen beyond that.

But I'd bought myself a little more time—and, *Theos mou*, I wanted to experience this again. And again. Without angst or acrimony.

Even now, with my limbs weak from their physical and emotional expenditure, hunger was slowly gathering force, anticipation adding fuel to a fire which didn't seem in a hurry to burn itself out. And if all it took was a simple recounting of my year, where was the harm?

I pushed away the voice urging caution and when I opened my mouth the words that tumbled out surprised even me.

'My grandmother was a feminists' feminist. She hated every aspect of a patriarchy that dictated what she could and couldn't do. She especially hated it when my grandfather died and everyone expected her to remarry because she had a young daughter to care for.'

I caught the edge of Ax's puzzled frown and couldn't help the smile that tugged at my lips.

'She never did remarry, but after she lost her house she was forced to live with my parents. I grew up in the shadows of her rebellion. She urged me to stand my ground. To question everything.'

His frown cleared, a droll look entering his grey eyes. 'Ah. I see.'

'Needless to say she butted heads with my father almost on a daily basis.'

Ax tensed. Not wanting the mood tarnished, I passed my hand over his chest—a soothing gesture that worked with Andreos but might not work with his father. My breath caught when he exhaled after a handful of seconds.

'Anyway, I found out on my wedding day that

she'd left me an envelope. My mother was to give it to me when she thought I needed it.'

A trace of regret flashed across his face. 'She thought you'd need it the day you married me.'

It wasn't a question, more of an acceptance of how things had turned out.

I shrugged. 'Besides my father, none of us knew much about you. What little I knew before we met at the altar I found out online,' I said, recognising but unable to stop the hint of censure in my tone.

The regret in his eyes deepened as he nodded. 'I accept that. So your father really kept you in the dark about everything?'

'Yes. And it wasn't anything new. He did that most of my life.'

'Why?'

The whisper of family shame slithered over my skin. 'Surely you've heard the rumours?'

'I prefer facts to rumours,' he stated.

I didn't bother to ask what he'd heard. I wanted this discussion over as quickly as possible.

'My mother left home when I was fifteen. She'd met another man and was planning on leaving my father. But they were involved in an accident. The man died. My mother survived— obviously—but she suffered a spine injury and… Well, you've seen her. My father brought her back home and promised to take care of her—under certain conditions.'

The hand that had been lazily trailing through my hair froze. 'It seems your father makes a habit of using people's misfortunes against them.'

I couldn't deny that truth. And when Ax used his hold to gently propel my gaze up to his I couldn't hide it from him.

Whatever he saw in my face made him exhale again. 'I used to think that was an encompassing Petras family trait,' he murmured.

'*Used* to?' Did that mean he'd changed his mind? That he *wasn't* tarring me with the same brush as my father any more?

He continued to stare at me for a long stretch. 'You're nothing like him. You have a formidable inner strength that he doesn't—clearly inherited from your grandmother,' he said.

The low, gruff words opened up a fountain of emotion inside me that stopped my breath, especially when he brushed his lips over mine, as if wanting to seal the words in.

Getting carried away would have been so easy, but I forced myself to pull back. 'Anyway, I moved from under my father's thumb to under yours without any intermission—'

He stiffened, his face growing a shade paler. 'Under my thumb? I made you feel like that?'

I shrugged. 'You dictated where I would live. How I would live. Without giving me a say. So when you told me to find a way... I did.'

His jaw tightened and after a moment he nodded. 'I don't blame you for staging a rebellion. I would have in your shoes too. Perhaps not with anonymity but...that's understandable considering my reaction to our marriage.'

Tears prickled my eyes, threatening to spill at the thought that he was seeing things from my side. 'Anyway, my grandmother's letter left details of a Swiss bank account in my name. I went to Switzerland to see what it was all about. She'd left me the means to live under a new identity if I chose. There was also a box with some of her things in it.'

'That's how you were able to live without detection for a year?' he said.

I nodded. 'I think she meant me to use it more as a way to rebel against my father than a way—'

'For you to escape your new husband?' he finished with terse amusement.

'Either way, it seemed like a sign.'

A touch of hardness entered his eyes. 'Leaving your husband tearing his hair out for a year.'

'You weren't my husband. You especially weren't interested in being one the morning after the wedding. You married me to save your precious company, so don't pretend my absence caused you any personal slight or even—heaven forbid—any *anxiety*!'

'You carried my name. You were supposed to be under my care. Believe me, your disappearance was punishment enough—especially when I was left imagining the worst,' he rasped in a raw tone.

Plastered to him as I was, I felt the shudder that shook his frame, and his set jaw and the flash of bleakness in his eyes spoke to a vulnerability I'd never have imagined him capable of until tonight.

I stopped breathing, because… No, I hadn't quite thought about it. 'It wasn't just our forced marriage, Axios. My father was threatening my mother too.'

Fury flashed in his eyes. 'What?'

'He wanted to keep me in line through her. But she made me promise I wouldn't stay if I was unhappy. It all got a bit too much.'

'Did he carry out his threat?'

I shook my head. 'I'm guessing he was too busy playing with his windfall.'

The monthly phone calls with my mother had assured me she was okay, and had been all the wind beneath my wings I'd needed to stay away.

He bit out a tight curse and threw an arm over his forehead. 'Your father has a lot to answer for, but he's saved himself a trouncing by leaving your mother alone,' he growled. After a moment, his gaze pierced mine again. 'My investigators eventually traced your flight from Greece to Switzerland and assured me that my wife had simply chosen to run away of her own accord. At least now I know how you managed to avoid detection after you left Geneva, but perhaps you'd be so kind as to finish telling me where you went?'

The pulse of anguish still underlined his anger, but knowing it wasn't directed at me made it easier to finish my retelling.

'I took a train to Strasbourg and then wandered through Europe for a time before heading to South-East Asia. After that I made my way through Africa.'

All the while keeping in touch with Dr Trudeau and praying for my baby's continued health.

'When did you know you were pregnant with Andreos?' he rasped.

My stomach hollowed out in remembrance, and it took every ounce of self-control not to show how that fateful day still affected me. How the possibility that I would never meet my child had

left me broken and sobbing for one day straight,
until the fervent prayers had begun.

'I found out early. In Switzerland.'

He waited, his gaze imploring me for more.
But I had nothing more to give. Nothing that
wouldn't see the precious time I had left with
Andreos compromised.

And it would be. It was clear Axios was deeply
possessive and protective of his son. Over the
past few days I'd learned just how meticulous
and all-powerful he could be. I couldn't afford
for the time I had with my baby to be compromised.

Or, on the flipside, he simply wouldn't care.

Pain snaked through me, dulling my heartbeat.
No, he was better off not knowing.

'Why Kenya?' he asked, tugging me back to
the present.

'Because I was seven months pregnant when
I got there. Because I loved it there and knew
I wouldn't be able to travel. I chose to stay and
have Andreos there.'

Again, he lapsed into contemplative silence,
those piercing grey eyes pinning me to the bed.
Then, 'Thank you for telling me,' he said simply. Gruffly.

Tears prickled. To hide them, I lowered my
head until our lips were a whisper apart. He

didn't protest. His eyes simply went molten and his hard body stirred beneath mine as I closed the gap and helped myself to the magic of his kiss.

He allowed my exploration for a minute. Allowed the tentative probe and the slide of my tongue against his in a deeper kiss while the hand around my waist moved in a slow caress up and down my back, until he boldly cupped my bottom and brought me into brazen contact with his impressive arousal.

Then he flipped me over and took complete control, effectively emptying my brain of everything but the naked desire snaking through my body, setting me alight with a need so acute all I could do was let it wholly consume me.

Nevertheless, his warning ricocheted in my head long after our bodies had cooled. Long after his deep, steady breathing indicated sleep.

Because telling myself I didn't care what my actions had caused Axios after I took up the fight for my health, that I wasn't important enough to cause a ripple in his existence, didn't quite ring true in my head. I cared. Even if marrying him and taking his name had been a transaction dictated by my father for financial gain, our coming together had produced a son. And that mattered.

Whether I liked it or not, Axios mattered to me. More than perhaps was wise.

The intensifying ache inside that reminded me I might have less time than I imagined added to the turmoil churning inside me, keeping me awake as dawn approached. Eventually mental exhaustion won out, and I fell into a sleep fuelled with pleasure and pain, blissful happiness and acute sadness.

Thankfully I was in a state of happiness when I resurfaced from sleep to the sound of a cooing baby.

'*Kalimera*, my angel,' I murmured, my drowsy awakening made all the better by my sweet baby's enthusiastic babble and the innocent smell of his freshly bathed body.

Eyes still closed, I felt my heart bursting with a joy that widened my smile.

'He's been very patient as he waited for his mama to wake, but I fear that state is about to be over,' drawled the deep, masculine voice of my baby's father.

My eyes flew open, the reminder of where I was and what had transpired last night fracturing my smile as I encountered the arresting image of a rudely vibrant Axios, one hand propping up his head and the other resting lightly on his son's stomach.

Andreos, his curious gaze switching between his father's face, mine, and just about every bright object it could touch upon, wriggled with impatience and babbled some more before letting out a cry that signalled he was well and truly done with waiting to be fed.

My lungs flattened with surprise and an unexpectedly sharp yearning as Ax shifted onto his back, lifted his son and held him aloft, a drop-dead gorgeous smile breaking out on his face as father and son stared at each other.

'You've made it this far, *o moro mou*. Give it another half-minute and you will be rewarded, hmm?' he teased.

I sat up, unable to help my blush and self-consciousness at the reminder that I was naked under the sheets.

After anointing his son's forehead with a gentle kiss, Axios turned to watch me sit up and arrange the pillows around me in preparation to feed an increasingly impatient Andreos.

When I was settled, Axios handed him over. And, just like last night, he didn't seem in a hurry to leave. In fact, he settled back on his pillow, his gaze unashamedly fixed on me as I settled our son at my breast.

Sunlight streamed through the partially opened curtain, bathing the parts of Axios I could see in mouthwatering relief—mainly his very naked, very chiselled torso. The effort it took to drag my gaze away and avoid the incisive eyes was depressingly monumental.

'I… What time is it?'

'It's a little after nine,' he answered, reaching out to caress his son's bare, plump foot. 'You were out of it when the monitor signalled that Andreos was awake. Sophia was about to give him a bottle, but I thought I'd bring him to you instead.'

I nodded, my throat clogging at the picture of togetherness and domestic bliss his words painted. Before I could stop myself, might-have-beens crowded my heart and I stared down at Andreos, painfully aware of Ax's presence in the pictures that filled my mind.

A little desperately, I reminded myself that this was all temporary. A short stretch of time to enjoy with my son before—

'Calypso?'

I blinked, unable to stop myself from being compelled to meet his gaze.

His eyes narrowed and he waited a beat before asking, 'What's wrong?'

I shook my head. 'It's nothing. I'm just a little tired, that's all.'

His shuttered gaze said he knew I was being

evasive. But he let it go. 'Not too tired to spend a few hours out of the city, I hope?'

Surprised, I stared at him. 'Out of the city?'

He nodded. 'I thought we could fly to Agistros for the afternoon. Agatha will organise a picnic for us and we'll spend a little time by the water.'

'Why?' I blurted.

He tensed slightly. 'On the rare occasion that I find myself with free time, I wish to spend it with our son. With you. I thought you might enjoy it. Am I wrong?'

I flushed. 'I... No.'

I'd planned nothing except spending a lazy day with Andreos. But the thought that Axios had plans, that he wanted to include us, kicked a wild little thrill into my bloodstream. A *dangerous* thrill. One I needed to nip in the bud sooner rather than later.

'I was planning on heading down to the beach here, but one beach is as good as any other, I suppose.'

A sly smile tilted one corner of his lip. 'I beg to differ. The beaches on Agistros rival the best in the world.'

My cheeky need to tease grew irresistible. 'According to *you*.'

His smile widened. 'Since I own it, my opinion is the only one that counts.'

The statement was so unapologetically arrogant I laughed. The sound seemed to arrest him, his eyes turning that molten shade that sent heat pulsing through my blood as we stared at each other.

'I believe this is the first time I've heard you laugh,' he rasped, his gaze raking over my face to settle brazenly on my mouth, almost effortlessly calling up another blush that suffused my face. 'I like it.'

Without warning his hand rose, his fingers trailing down one hot cheek and along my jaw before dropping down to recapture his son's foot.

Something heavy and urgent and profound shifted inside me. The thought that I didn't know this facet of the man I'd married and that I wanted to hit me square in the midriff, before flaring a deep yearning towards all the dark corners of my heart.

My smile felt frayed around the edges as I fought to maintain my composure, fought not to blurt out another prayer for things I didn't deserve.

I'd been given so much already.

Gloom wormed through my heart, the fear of what lay ahead and of fighting an uphill battle I might not win casting shadows over the gift of another day.

I was still struggling to banish it when a knock came on the door.

'Ah, right on time,' he murmured.

With another heart-stopping smile Axios launched himself out of bed. Naked and gladiator-like in all his glory, he walked across the suite, stopping long enough to pull on a dark dressing robe before heading for the door.

He returned a minute later, wheeling a solid silver trolley loaded with breakfast dishes. Bypassing his side of the bed, he stopped the trolley close to me before hitching up a thigh and settling himself next to me.

I tried and failed not to watch him pour coffee for himself, tea for me, and lift a large, succulent bowl of ripe strawberries.

He waited until I'd put Andreos over my shoulder and begun rubbing his back to elicit a burp before he shifted closer. Dipping one end of a strawberry into a bowl of rich cream, he leaned forward and then held the plump fruit against my lip.

'Taste.' His voice was deep, low. Hypnotising.

I leaned forward, parted my lips and took the offering. He watched me chew with the kind of rapt attention that could wreak havoc with a woman's sensibilities. Only after I'd swallowed did he help himself to a piece—minus the cream.

He alternated between feeding me and himself until the bowl was empty, and then he set about piling more food on a plate.

'I can't eat all that,' I protested as I laid a very satisfied Andreos down beside me.

Axios shrugged, setting the tray in my lap. 'Our son is very demanding. And I get the feeling that state is only going to get more challenging. You'll need all the advantages you can get.'

About to tell him there was nothing I was anticipating more, the words stuck in my throat, and a bolt of heartache clenched my heart in a merciless vice.

Thankfully Axios was in the process of lifting a newspaper from a side pocket of the trolley, granting me a scant few seconds to get my emotions under control before he straightened and flicked the paper open.

Then a different sort of tension assailed me.

Seeing the pictures gracing the front page, I felt my gut twist. While I'd known we'd be under scrutiny last night, it hadn't occurred to me that we'd actually make front-page news.

The first picture had been taken when we'd first entered the ballroom. With our heads close together, Ax's masculine cheek almost touching mine, it hinted at an edgy intimacy between us that was almost too private.

From the look on Axios's face, he didn't feel the same.

He turned the page and my insides churned faster. There were more pictures, including some of us on the balcony, his hand splayed on my back, right before he pulled me in for that toe-curling kiss.

Axios stared at the pictures with something close to smug satisfaction.

'Did you know we were being photographed?' I asked, biting into a piece of ham-layered toast and concentrating on stirring my tea so I wouldn't have to look at the picture. At how the sight of Axios in a tuxedo continued to wreak havoc with my equilibrium. Nor face the fact that a very large part of me was wondering what true intimacy with this man whose name I'd taken would feel like.

He shrugged. 'I suspected we might be.'

That he was very much okay with it—had perhaps even wanted us to be photographed—was evident.

'And has it achieved what you meant it to?' I needed the reminder that this was all for a reason. For a definitive purpose which *didn't* include getting carried away with fairy tales.

With a flick of his fingers he folded the paper and picked up his coffee. 'If you mean are my business partners back on board, then, yes. But let's not rest on our laurels just yet,' he said.

Did that mean more socialising? More moments like those on the balcony? And why didn't that fill me with horror? Why was my belly tingling with thrilling anticipation?

Questions and sensations stayed with me through a quick shower and lingered while I chose a bikini set, pulled a floaty spaghetti-strap sundress over it and slipped my feet into stylish wedge shoes.

Stepping out to join Axios and Andreos two hours later, on the landscaped lawn that led to the helipad, I noticed we were flying in a different, larger chopper.

Axios caught my questioning look. 'This one is more insulated. To better protect Andreos's delicate eardrums,' he said, casting an indulgent glance at the baby nestled high in the crook of his arm.

Of course he *would* have a special helicopter that catered for babies!

With the sensation of having woken up in an alternative universe from which I couldn't escape, I walked beside him to the aircraft.

The trip, unlike last time, flew by, and before I knew it we were skimming the beaches of Agistros, the azure waters of the island sparkling in the sunlight.

The villa was just as breathtaking as it had been a year ago, and this time, without deep trepidation blinding me, I was better able to appreciate it. Granted, there were other equally precarious emotions simmering beneath my skin, but just for today I let the dazed dream wash over me, revelling in simply *being* as Axios stepped out of the helicopter, reached to help me out and took control of Andreos's travel seat.

Expecting tension, in light of the way I'd departed the villa the last time, I breathed a sigh of relief when the staff, headed by Agatha, spilled out with welcoming smiles. It was obvious that news of Andreos had travelled as they cooed over him.

When Agatha carried him off to the kitchen to supervise the picnic preparation, I drifted into the living room with Axios.

Dressed in the most casual attire I'd seen him in so far—high-spec cargo trousers and a navy rugby shirt—he nevertheless still looked as if he'd stepped straight off the cover of a magazine.

To keep myself from shamelessly ogling him, I drifted over to the set of framed photos on one of the many antique cabinets gracing the room. There was a slightly faded one of an old man, his distinguished and distinctive features announcing him as Theodore Xenakis. Ax's grandfather. The man who'd been forced under duress to make an agreement that had changed lives—including mine.

Perhaps it wasn't the best choice of subject matter to bring up on what was meant to be a lazy day by the beach. But after hearing Axios open up about his father, I wanted to know more. Yearned to learn what had formed the man whose name I bore.

Once we'd made our way down to a private beach, tucked into the most stunning bay I'd ever seen in my life, I found myself asking, 'Did your grandfather ever live here on Agistros?'

He stiffened, but his tension eased almost immediately. 'In the latter part of his life, yes.'

There was more to that statement. 'Why? I mean, I've seen your family. I know you're dispersed all over Athens, and on several family-owned islands. I also know that Agistros belongs to you. So why did he live here? Did he need care?'

For the longest time I thought he wouldn't answer. When he did reply, his tone was low. Deep. As if remembering was painful.

'Before his company fell on hard times my grandfather invested in real estate and gifted islands to every family member. Neo has an island twenty miles from here.'

At the mention of his brother it was my turn to stiffen. 'I don't think Neo likes me.'

Ax's eyes glinted, a hard kind of amusement shifting in their depths. 'He's going through a…a situation.'

'A "situation"?'

'Something's been taken from him that he wasn't quite ready to part with,' he said cryptically.

I frowned. 'Someone's stolen from him?'

'In a manner of speaking.'

Recalling our conversation, I frowned. 'A woman?'

Again, dark amusement twisted Ax's lips. 'Yes. And a formidable one, I hear.'

Realising he wasn't going to elaborate, I pressed gently, 'So…about your grandfather…?'

A trace of bleakness whispered across his face. 'He left Kosima, his favourite island, for many reasons. But mainly because the strain of trying to save his company took a toll on his family, especially my grandmother. After she died we didn't deem it wise for him to remain on Kosima by himself. So he came to stay here.'

I wanted to probe deeper, find out why the once booming Xenakis empire had swan-dived to the brink of bankruptcy three years before his grandfather had died. But I held my tongue because I suspected my own family had had a hand in the Xenakis family's misfortune. Also, that flash of bleakness resonated inside me, his pain echoing mine.

Not wanting the day ruined by revisiting the animosity between our families, I stared at the stunning horizon, a different urge overtaking me. 'I wish I could paint this,' I murmured, almost to myself.

Ax turned to me. 'When was the last time you painted?'

Unsurprised that he knew of my passion, I answered, 'All through my pregnancy, and a short while after Andreos was born.'

'Why didn't you pursue your painting before?'

I shrugged. 'There wasn't much call for it on Nicrete.'

His silence was contemplative. 'You wanted to do something with it in Athens. Do you still want to?' he asked, a trace of guilt in his voice.

Not if I don't have much time left.

'Perhaps not full-time but…yes.'

'I would like to see you paint.'

Something melted inside me and I couldn't help my gasp. 'You would?'

He gave an abrupt nod. 'If you would allow it…very much.'

Again something tugged inside me, harder this time—a feeling of my world tilting, making me sway towards him.

To counteract it before I did something supremely unwise, I tugged my dress over my head. 'I'm going for a swim.'

With every step from sand to sea I felt his gaze burn into my skin, heating me up from the inside out. Thigh-deep, I dived into the cool, exquisite water, hoping it would wash away the discordant emotions zinging through me.

This really shouldn't be difficult. All we had to do was exist in the same space until I was absolutely certain Andreos would be safe and cared for, before I returned to Dr Trudeau in Switzerland to face my fate.

All I had to do was prevent myself from falling under Ax's spell. Surely it wasn't that hard?

Yes, it is. I feel more for him with every passing minute!

The weight of that verdict was so disturbing I didn't sense his presence until the second before he wrapped a strong arm around my waist.

His hair was slicked back, throwing the sharp, majestic angles of his face into stunning relief. Droplets of water sparkled on his face, a particularly tempting one clinging to his upper lip, evoking in me a wild need to lick it off.

'Andreos!' I protested.

'He's fine,' he said with hard gruffness as he pulled me closer, tangled my legs with his.

I looked over and sure enough our son was well-insulated by plump pillows, shaded by a large umbrella, happily playing with his rattle.

'Calypso...'

My name was a thick demand I couldn't resist. And when he pulled me into his arms and slanted his sensual lips across mine I gave in, my conflicting thoughts melting away under the heat of mounting passion.

Afterwards we returned and spread out on the blankets. A trace of trepidation returned, tingeing the closeness wrapping itself around us, a closeness I wanted to hang on to despite the uncertainty lurking in the future.

Because this version of Axios, who wanted to see me paint, who had opened up about his grandfather, was a version who could so easily worm his way into my heart.

On the Monday morning after our first trip to Agistros I arrived downstairs to find six high-spec easels and an assortment of expensive paints and brushes. Stunned, I blinked away tears as Axios presented them to me.

'You…you shouldn't have.'

He shook his head. 'You've denied your passion long enough,' he said. 'A year longer than necessary because of me,' he added heavily.

Next he organised special transportation for my mother to visit. Having not seen each other for a year, our reunion was tearful, her joy over her grandson boundless.

Seeing her, reassuring myself that she was all right despite the pain still clouding her eyes, lifted a weight off my shoulders. And that melting sensation returned full force when Axios set out to charm her—a ploy that worked to dissipate the lingering tension between them once and for all.

From my father I heard nothing. And, frankly, it didn't overly bother me.

After that our lives fell into a pattern.

Weekdays were spent at the villa in Athens, with at least three evenings of the week spent at one social engagement or another, which inevitably made front-page news, while Saturday and Sunday were spent on Agistros.

It was almost idyllic—the only fly in the ointment Dr Trudeau's increasingly urgent emails and the knowledge that now I was assured of

Ax's complete devotion to our son I had no cause to put my health issues on hold.

It was on one weekend a few weeks later, in the place we'd now designated our picnic spot, when he glanced over at me as he reclined on a shaded lounger with a sleepy Andreos dozing on his bare chest. Father and son were besotted with each other, the growing bond between them a source of untold joy to me.

'I'm flying to Bangkok on Tuesday for business.'

Since he never discussed his business arrangements with me I met his gaze in surprise, unwilling to expose the sharp sting that had arrived and lodged in my midriff. 'Okay...'

'You and Andreos can come with me.'

The swiftness with which the sting eased was dismaying—and a little terrifying. Enough to trigger a waspish response. 'Is that a question or a command?'

The flash of flint in his eyes stunned me. Hard on its heels came the realisation that I much preferred his blinding smiles. The sexy growls when he was aroused. Even his sometimes mocking tones.

Theos, I'd fallen into a highly dangerous state of lust, complacency, and a host of other things I didn't want to name. One in particular had been gaining momentum, clamouring for attention I was too afraid to give it. It was there when I woke. It blanketed me before I fell asleep and teased my dreams. It was there now, pulsing beneath my skin as Ax's gaze locked on mine and another blinding smile made an appearance.

'It's whichever you find easiest to comply with.'

For some absurd reason my heart flipped over even as I wondered whether he was asking me along because the thought of being separated from us for any length of time was disagreeable to him or because of appearances.

His expression was mostly unreadable, but there was something there. A touch of apprehension I'd never seen before. And, though it was highly unwise to latch on to it, I found myself leaning towards it, indulging myself in the idea that he *cared* whether I agreed or not.

'How long is this trip going to last?'

'It's to finalise a new airline deal I've been working on for a year. It's been challenging at times, so I expect both sides will want to celebrate after the deed is done. Prepare to stay for the better part of a week. Did you travel to Thailand on your trip?' he asked, but his almost flippant query didn't fool me for one second.

Axios was a master at subtle inquisition. Over

the past weeks he'd dropped several questions unexpectedly.

'No. My coin-flip landed in favour of Indonesia instead of Thailand, so I went to Bali.'

'Then this will be your chance to explore another country,' he replied smoothly, despite the trace of tension in the air.

Andreos chose that moment to make his displeasure at the charged atmosphere known. Axios absently soothed a hand down his small back, but his eyes remained fixed on me.

When I reached for him Ax handed him over. Then he stayed sitting, his elbows resting on his knees.

'Will you come with me?' he asked, his eyes boring into mine.

And because that undeniable yearning for *more* wouldn't stop—because I craved this...*togetherness* more than I craved my next breath—I answered, 'Yes.'

CHAPTER NINE

TIME IS RUNNING OUT...

The unnerving sensation that time was slipping through my fingers had arrived like a thief in the night and stayed like an unwanted guest, permeating my every interaction with Calypso. I couldn't put my finger on *why* and nor did I have a clear-cut solution.

The sensation left me off-kilter and scowling as I climbed the steps into my plane two days later.

A lot of things I'd believed to be cut and dried had become nebulous in the past few weeks. The idea of marriage...of *staying* married, for instance...didn't evoke the same amount of resistance it had done a year or even a month ago. As for being a father...

Thoughts of Andreos immediately soothed a fraction of the chaos inside me. My son's existence had brought a deeper purpose to my life I wouldn't have believed possible had I not experienced it for myself. The chance to pass on my heritage to him, to teach him about the sacrifices his grandfather had made filled a bleak corner of my soul.

As for his mother…

The warmth I'd enjoyed with her over the past few weeks, watching her joy in painting and simply basking in the unit she and Andreos presented had subtly altered, leaving me with more questions than answers. Even more acute was the feeling of exposure after revealing so much of myself and the anguish her family's actions had caused mine.

Yes, but only one member of her family…not all of them…

My chest twinged with another sting of guilt. I'd learned from my grandfather's mistakes, applied his good mentoring to my life and avoided the bad. Shouldn't the same apply to Calypso? Especially when she'd been caught in the same web of greed as I had?

The urge to hash this out with her grew stronger. And yet the fear of repeating the mistakes of last year, driving her away, stopped me.

It didn't help that over the last day or so she'd seemed under the weather, thereby curtailing any serious conversation I'd felt inclined to have or my reaching for that final resort of last resorts— tugging her into my arms in the dark of night and letting the mindless bliss of having her melt every fractious thought away.

Harmony and unstinting passion—it was a combination I would never have associated with her a few weeks ago, but I now craved to have it back.

My gaze fell on her as I entered the living area of the plane. She was chatting to one of the attendants, her alluring smile sparking heat in my bloodstream as she nodded to whatever was being said.

Unable to help myself, I let my gaze trail over her. The cream form-fitting jumpsuit caressed her luscious body from shoulder to ankle, its emphasis of her supple behind and lush breasts drying my mouth and reminding me that it had been three long days since I'd had the pleasure of her body.

The attendant departed, and as Calypso turned to sit I noticed the top buttons securing the front were left undone to reveal her impressive cleavage. My groin stirred harder and it was all I could do not to give a bad-tempered, frustrated groan.

I approached, dropping into the seat opposite her. She held Andreos like a buffer, her gaze stubbornly avoiding mine even though she was aware of my presence.

'The silent treatment isn't going to work where we're headed. You do know that, don't you?'

The blue eyes that finally deigned to meet mine were shadowed, her face still showing a hint of the paleness that raised an entirely new set of ruffled emotions inside me.

'Don't worry, Axios. I'll put on the appropriate performance when needed.'

Even her voice had lost a trace of that passionate lustre that fired up my blood.

'Are you all right?' The words were pulled from a deep, *needy* part of me.

Her eyes widened, then she nodded abruptly and her gaze dropped to Andreos. 'I'm fine. Just a slight…stomach ache.'

The unsettling sensation deepened, the niggling feeling that I was missing something escalating. 'Did you take anything for it? I'll get the attendant to bring you—'

She shook her head hastily when I reached for the intercom button, but I didn't miss the shadow that crossed her face, the knuckles that whitened in her lap.

'It's… I'm fine, Ax. I think I'll go and lie down with Andreos for a while after we take off.'

True to her word, the moment we reached cruising altitude she unbuckled herself, rose, and headed to the back of the plane with Andreos.

The urge to follow, to demand answers to the teeming questions ricocheting in my brain, was so strong I clenched my gut against the power of it.

I stayed put, forcing rationality over impulse. I had business to take care of, conference calls to make. And yet somewhere on that endless to-do list the looming issue of our agreement ticked louder.

An agreement I'd lately found myself re-examining with growing dissatisfaction.

Restlessness drove me to my feet. At the bar, I poured myself a cognac and tossed it back, hoping the bracing heat would knock some sense into me. All it did was emphasise the expanding hollow inside me and quicken this alien need demanding satisfaction.

Setting the glass down, I started to walk back to my seat—and then, unsurprised, I found myself moving towards the back of the plane.

After my soft knock elicited no response I turned the door handle. Lamps were dimmed, the window shades drawn, but still I saw them. Both asleep.

One with small, chubby arms thrown above his head in innocent abandon.

My son. My world.

The other curled on her side with one arm

braced protectively over Andreos and the other
draped over her belly.

My wife.

But not for much longer. Unless I took steps
to do something about it.

Resolution slid home like a key in a lock I
didn't even realise needed opening. Now I did—
now the possibility of *more* beckoned with a
promise I didn't want to deny.

Shaking out a light throw, I tucked it over both
of them, then stepped back.

Calypso made a distressed sound in her sleep,
an anxious twitch marring her brow for a second before it smoothed out and her breathing
grew steady.

Was her stomach still bothering her? I frowned
as that niggling returned.

My hand clenched over the door handle.

Were her secrets disturbing her sleep? Could
that be the last stumbling block I needed to overcome to make this marriage real? If so, could I
live with it?

The breath locked in my lungs was released,
along with the bracing realisation that, regardless of what the secret was, it needn't get in our
way. If she was prepared not to let it.

Very much aware that several things hung in
the balance, I stepped out, shut the door behind

me and returned to the living room. But through all my strategising and counter-strategising my resolution simply deepened.

My grandfather had sacrificed and nearly lost everything in his dealings with one Petras.

But perhaps it was time to draw a line underneath all that, let acrimony stay in the past where it belonged.

Perhaps it was time to strike yet another bargain.

A more permanent one.

Thailand was magical.

Or as magical as a place could be when I knew that dark shadows crept ever closer. Knew that my stolen time was rapidly dwindling away.

It marred my ability to enjoy fully the sheer magnificence of our tropical paradise except on canvas, with the paints Axios had supplied me with, which conversely helped in keeping my true state under wraps for a little longer.

The discomfort in my abdomen which he had erroneously assumed was my period kept him from the jaw-droppingly stunning master suite of our Bangkok villa at night. And when we were required to make an appearance together at one of the many events marking the successful merger of Xenakis Aeronautics and a major

Thai-owned airline he was painfully solicitous, showering me with the kind of attention that made the tabloid headlines screech with joy.

The kind that made my heart swell with a foolish longing that I knew would make the inevitable break all the more agonising.

The kind he'd showered me with over the last few weeks but that now came with a speculative look in his eyes. As if he was trying to solve a puzzle. As if he was trying to make our situation *work*.

But my guilt at the subterfuge was nothing compared to the grief tearing my heart to shreds at the thought of leaving Andreos.

When, after four days in Bangkok, Axios announced that we were relocating to Kamala in Phuket for the remaining three days, for a delayed honeymoon, I knew I couldn't hide from my feelings any longer.

I was in love with Axios.

Even knowing he didn't feel the same couldn't diminish the knowledge that I'd been falling since that night on the balcony. Since I'd agreed to *for now*. But, contrarily, accepting my true feelings meant I couldn't in good conscience burden him or my precious baby with the battle ahead.

I was in love with my husband. And to spare him our marriage had to end.

Tucked inside the bamboo shelter of a rainforest shower, I gave in to the silent sobs tearing my heart to pieces, letting the warm spray wash my tears away. When I was wrung out, I carefully disguised the tell-tale signs of my distress with subtle make-up before leaving the suite.

In bare feet and a floaty white dress that whispered softly around my body, I approached the sound of infant giggles, a deep, sexy voice and the playful splash of water.

Axios was enjoying a lazy swim with Andreos. And, as much as I wanted to stop and frame the beautiful picture father and son made, so I could carry it in my heart, I knew my emotions were far too close to the surface to risk detection.

Instead I made my way past the pool and through the glass hallway that led to another stunning wing of the multi-tiered luxury villa. To the special place I'd discovered on our arrival.

The suspended treehouse was accessed by a heavy plank and rope bridge from the second level of the villa and a broad ladder from the level below. I took the walkway, enjoying the swaying movement that made me feel as if I was dancing on air, and entered the wide space laid out with polished wooden floors, wide rectangular windows and a roped-off platform that gave magnificent views of the Andaman Sea and the Bay of Bengal.

A riot of vivid colour brush-stroked the horizon, signalling the approach of night. Silently awed, and my breath held, I watched the colours settle into breathtaking layers of a purple and orange sunset.

I wasn't sure how long I stood there, lost in my turbulent thoughts, selfishly praying for things I couldn't have. And even when I sensed Axios's approach I didn't turn around, didn't give in to the raw need to fill my senses with the sight and sound of him.

Instead I gripped the rope barrier until my knuckles shrieked with just a fraction of the pain shredding my insides.

Whether he sensed my mood or not, Axios didn't speak either. But when he stopped behind me I felt the intensity of his presence. And when he slid an arm around my waist and engulfed me in the poignant scents of father and son I couldn't help the scalding tears that prickled my eyes.

With a soft moan I sagged into his hold, and the three of us stood on the platform, staring at the horizon as the bright orange ball of the sun dipped into the sea and a blanket of stars started to fill the sky.

'Come,' he said eventually, his voice low and deep. 'The chef is almost done preparing dinner. Let's go put our son to bed, hmm?'

Throat tight with locked emotion, I nodded, making sure to avoid his probing gaze as we made our back into the villa. After putting a dozing Andreos in his cot, we retraced our steps to the open terrace, where a candlelit dinner had been laid out.

There, Axios pulled out a chair and I sat, my stomach in knots and my heart bleeding, as I looked at the face of the man I was hopelessly in love with.

The man I could never have.

Theos mou, she was gorgeous.

The breath that had stalled in my lungs fought to emerge as I watched candlelight dance over her face and throat. Even the veil of melancholy shrouding her didn't detract from the captivating mix of fire and calm I wanted to experience for a very long time.

For ever.

Our three-course dinner had passed in stilted conversation, and our appetites had been non-existent. She'd refused dessert and I'd downed my aromatic espresso in one go.

But it was time.

Business pressures had forced this conversation to the back burner for the last four days. It was time to lay my cards on the table.

'About the divorce you requested: I would like to renegotiate...'

A vice tightened my sternum when wild panic flared in her eyes. The hand resting on the table began to tremble and she snatched it away, tucking it into her lap as she exhaled sharply. 'What do you mean, "renegotiate"? You gave me your word!'

For the first time I felt a visceral need to take it all back, to smash it to pieces and rebuild something new, something lasting from the rubble created from greed and blind lust. Because there was something more here. This... *distance* between us had cemented my belief that this wasn't just sex. That I'd fallen deeper, farther than even my imagination could fathom. Perhaps even into that dimension where Calypso could exist.

The thought of that ending...of never experiencing it or her at some point in the future... twisted in something close to agony inside me.

The state was further evidenced by the quiet panic this very argument was fuelling inside me—the fine trembles coursing through my body, taunting me with the possibility that this might be the one deal that eluded me. That my actions last year and since finding her on Bora Bora might have doomed me in her eyes. The very thought that I might fail where I'd succeeded at everything else. Everything that mattered...

No.

'I know what I promised, but I no longer think it's—'

'No!'

She surged to her feet, and the trembling in her hand seemed transmitted to her body as eyes steeped in turmoil centred on mine. But when she spoke her voice was firm, the most resolute I'd ever heard her. And that only twisted the knife in deeper. Because I sensed a dynamic shift in her the like of which I'd never experienced before.

She seemed to falter for a moment, her hand sliding to her stomach, before she shook her head. 'You made a promise, Axios, and I'm going to have to insist you deliver on that promise.'

That gesture...

'Tell me why, Calypso. Give me a reason why you won't even hear me out,' I challenged, feeling the ground slip away beneath my feet even as I rose and faced her across the dinner table.

* * *

'Why?' he grated again when words failed to emerge from my strangled throat in time to answer his question.

His features were changing from a determined sort of cajoling to frighteningly resolute.

'Are you pregnant?' he added hoarsely, and there was a blaze of what looked like hope in his eyes as they dropped to my stomach.

'What? No, I'm not pregnant,' I blurted, dropping my hand.

Was that disappointment on his face?

'Can we take a breath and discuss this rationally?' he asked.

The desire to do just that—to let him talk me into dreaming about an impossible future—was so heart-wrenchingly tempting it took the sharp bite of my nails into my palm to stop agreement spilling from my lips.

'No. I'm all talked out, Axios. All I want now is action. For you to stick to your word and… and let me go.'

His grey eyes went molten for a handful of seconds before his jaw clenched tight. 'Why? We've proved in the last few weeks that we're completely compatible. As parents to Andreos. And in the bedroom.'

Desperately, I shook my head. 'We…we can

love Andreos as much together as apart. As for the bedroom…it's just sex. Basing a marriage on it is delusional.'

'I beg to differ. The kind of compatibility we have is unique. Don't be so dismissive of it. Besides, how would you know? I'm the only lover you've ever had,' he tossed in arrogantly.

And he would be the only one for me. 'That still doesn't mean I want to give up everything for the sake of—'

A throat clearing on the edge of the terrace interrupted me. Sophia, now Andreos's official nanny, had travelled with us to Thailand, and she looked supremely nervous.

'What is it?' Axios demanded.

'There's a call from Switzerland for Kyria Xenakis. They say they've been trying to reach you.'

I felt the blood draining from my face as Axios frowned. *Dr Trudeau, tired of waiting for me to contact him.*

'Tell them I'll call back tomorrow,' I said hastily.

The second Sophia hurried away, Axios's gaze sharpened on me. 'Why are you getting a call from Switzerland?'

'I still have business there,' I replied, hoping he'd let it go.

For a terse moment I thought he'd push, but then he sighed. 'What were you going to say before? For the sake of what, Calypso?'

For the sake of unrequited love.

Mercifully, the words remained locked deep inside me, the only hint spilling out in my strained voice as I fought to remain upright, to fight for this vital chance to do this on my own terms.

'I can't—I don't *want* anything long-term. I want to be free.'

To fight for the chance to return whole. Even to dream of starting again with a clean slate.

Hope dried up as Ax's face turned ashen, his eyes darkening with something raw and potent. Something I wasn't sure I wanted to decipher, because it resembled the helpless yearning inside me.

But that couldn't be. Axios not only hated what my father had done to him, he despised what my family had done to his grandfather. I was the last person he could be contemplating hitching himself to for the long term. Which meant that whatever his proposal was it still had an end date. That even if Dr Trudeau had a sliver of hope for me I might not have a chance with Ax.

Nonetheless, temptation buffeted me until I had to hold on to the edge of the table to keep from falling into it.

'Free to live your life? What about our *son*, Calypso?' he demanded scathingly, his voice ragged. 'Do you intend to drag him along on another freedom jaunt? Are you so blinkered to his needs that you would rip him from me to satisfy your own needs?'

'Of course not!'

The searing denial was the final thread holding my emotions together. I felt the hot slide of tears and could do nothing to stop it. So I stood there, my world going into one final free fall, and set the words I despised but *needed* to say spilling free.

'He...he's happy in Athens. He's a Xenakis. You love him. He belongs with you. You can...' *Keep him. Love him. The way I might not be able to.*

The final words dried in my throat, the final selfless act of handing over my precious son unwilling to be given voice. But still he *knew.*

Knew and condemned me absolutely for it.

Brows clamped in horror, he stared at me. 'Are you—?' He stopped, shook his head in abject disbelief. 'You're leaving him behind? Your quest for freedom is so great that you intend to completely abandon your son?'

His voice was bleak, his eyes pools of bewilderment.

'Or it is something else, Calypso? Is it me? Have I not proved I can be a good husband, provide for you and our son?'

There was my chance. Say no and this would be over. Tell him he'd failed me and it would be done. But I couldn't. Because even if he didn't love me, he hadn't failed me.

'Please, Axios—'

'Please what?' he asked urgently, stalking around the table towards me. 'Make it easier for you to walk away from your child? From me?'

His chest rose and fell in uncharacteristic agitation, his eyes dark, dismal.

'I watched my grandfather's world crumble around him. You want me to let you do the same to mine?' he rasped jaggedly.

I squeezed my eyes shut. 'Please don't say that.'

'Why not?' he demanded, his expression hardening. 'You want easy? Let me make it simple for you. Take one step out through the front door and you will never set eyes on Andreos again. I will make it my mission to erase your name from his life. It will be as if you never even existed.'

Choked tears clogged my throat and my world turned inside out with sorrow.

'You would do that? Really?'

He hesitated, one hand rising to glide roughly over his mouth and jaw before he shook his head.

'Make me understand, Calypso. What could possibly be out there that you won't get with me? What could be more important to you than to care for our child? To watch him grow and thrive under our care?'

I pressed my lips together, the agony of keeping the naked truth locked inside me so it wouldn't stain Andreos killing me. 'My...my freedom. I want what I've wanted for as long as I can remember, Axios. I want to be free.'

For the longest time he simply stared in stark disbelief. Then his breath shuddered out. And with it the last of the bewilderment in his eyes. Now he saw how set I was on bringing this to an end, his jaw clenched in tight resolution.

'Is that your final decision?' he grated.

My balled fist rose from the table, rested on my abdomen and the possible time bomb ticking inside me. 'Yes. It is.'

'Very well. You'll hear from my lawyers before the week is out.'

My breath strangled to nothing. *It was over. Just like that?*

'Axios—'

'No!' His hand slashed through the air. 'There's no room for bargaining.'

And in that moment, presented with his bleak

verdict, I felt the words simply tumble out. 'I'm sick, Axios. I have a lump…in my cervix.'

He froze, his eyes widening with shock as he stumbled back a step. 'What?' he whispered, his face ashen.

'I suspected it last year—a few weeks before we married. The doctor in Switzerland who confirmed I was pregnant also confirmed the presence of the lump. My…my grandmother died of cervical cancer—'

'Why have you waited this long for treatment?' he railed.

'Andreos. I wanted to make sure he was safe. And loved.'

He went even paler, his eyes growing pools of horror and disbelief. 'You've known this…you've carried this for a year…and you didn't tell me?' he rasped, almost to himself as he gripped his nape with a shaky hand. 'Why? Because you were testing me? Because I let you down? Because you don't trust me?'

No! Because I love you. Because I can't let you both watch me die.

'Because I didn't want to put Andreos through what might happen. He was a miracle, Ax. I couldn't…didn't know if I could carry him to term, but once I knew I was pregnant I knew I had to *try*.'

'You found out about the lump the same day you found out you were carrying Andreos?' he asked, his voice still stark.

I nodded. 'I just… I couldn't lose him, Ax. I couldn't risk a biopsy to find out whether my prognosis was the same as my grandmother's. But I agreed to frequent scans that wouldn't harm the baby. When the first one showed that the pregnancy was stopping the lump from grow-ing—'

'You chose to stay pregnant,' he finished, awed disbelief in his voice.

I sniffed back tears and nodded again. 'You see, Andreos was a miracle in so many ways. Conceiving him bought me time, and once he was born… I just couldn't let him go.'

'But the lump is still there. It's causing you pain, isn't it?' he asked, even though the knowl-edge blazed in his eyes. 'That's why you touch your stomach. That's why you were unwell on the plane. And the timing of your return… That was your plan all along—to hand over Andreos and go off and fight this on your own?'

'Yes,' I answered simply. 'I've had one scan since Andreos was born. It showed a small growth rate. But it's…it's time for further tests. Axios, I watched my grandmother suffer in the last months of her life. I can't…*won't* put Andreos through that if that's what I'm facing. I *have* to leave. I would prefer it if you didn't fight me. But…what you said…about erasing me from his life—'

Axios cursed and shoved both hands through his hair. 'That was an idle threat. You'll always be his mother and he'll know you as such. He'll know your courage and what you did for him,' he intoned in a low, solemn voice.

At my sob of relief his lips firmed and he stared at me for an age. 'Andreos,' he said heavily, with a finality that struck real fear into me. 'He's the only reason you're doing this.'

It was a statement—as if he already knew the answer. He took a step back. Then another. Until an unpassable chasm yawned between us.

'Very well. If you've made your choice then so be it.'

I'd expected this to come, but still I stood in utter shock as Axios blazed one last searing look at me, then turned and stalked away.

Shock turned into numbing self-protection when, upon waking up alone in the master suite the next day, I learned from Sophia that Ax had left. That he'd left instructions for Andreos and I to return to Athens alone.

As if the staff knew things had changed dras- tically, from the moment we walked through the front door of the Athens villa the atmosphere seemed altered. The only one who thankfully remained oblivious was Andreos. Having mastered the art of rolling over, he was now determined to conquer sitting up in record time, and thus provided the only source of delight in the house.

In a bid to make the most of whatever time I had with him, before Ax returned, I all but banished poor Sophia as I greedily devoured every precious second.

Two days turned to three.

Then four.

And then came the news from the housekeeper that Ax was expected mid-afternoon.

The urge to delay my exit, to see his face one last time, pummelled me. But, knowing I couldn't delay the inevitable, I booked my flight to Switzerland. The bag I'd hastily packed while Andreos napped stood like a silent omen at the foot of my bed.

'The car's waiting, *kyria*,' Sophia informed me, her face wreathed in worry.

Unchecked tears streamed down my face as I leaned down and brushed my lips over Andreos' plump cheek. 'Promise me you'll look after him?' I managed through a clogged throat.

Sophia's anxious gaze searched mine. 'I... I promise. But, *kyria*—'

I shook my head, knowing I'd break down if this was prolonged. 'That's good enough for me. Thank you, Sophia.'

Bag in hand, I hurried out, flew down the stairs to the waiting car. Blind with tears, I didn't register his presence until the car was pulling away.

'I will allow those tears for now, *pethi mou*. But for what comes next I'll need that formidable resilience I've come to know and adore.'

CHAPTER TEN

'AXIOS! WHAT...WHAT are you doing here?'

His face was as gaunt and ashen as the last time I'd seen it. But in his eyes purpose and determination blazed in place of horrified anguish.

Even so, the sight of him shook me, his presence unearthing a cascade of emotions through me.

When he didn't answer, when all he seemed to want was to absorb every inch of my face, I tried again. 'I thought you'd gone...that I'd never see you again.'

His chest heaved in a mighty exhalation. 'I had to go,' he replied gruffly.

Despair and disappointment slashed me wide open. 'Oh. I understand.'

He gave a grating self-deprecating laugh that was chopped off halfway through. '*Do* you? Do you understand how utterly useless and powerless I felt? How I had to walk away because I knew I'd failed you again?'

'What? Why would you—?'

'We will dissect that later. But for now...' my breath caught as his thumb brushed away my tears, '…it's tearing me apart to see these tears,' he grated roughly.

Which only made them fall harder.

'Andreos… Leaving him…that's tearing *me* apart.'

'Just Andreos?'

The question was deep and low. But heavy with unspoken emotions.

I lifted my gaze to find him watching me with hawk-like intensity, his eyes burning with a new light. One that made my insides leap.

'Ax…'

Before I could answer his hand seized mine, his eyes steadfast on me.

'Will you give me the chance to make things right, Calypso? Trust me just for a little while?' he demanded with a hoarse plea.

About to answer, I paused as we pulled up at the private airstrip and stopped next to his plane. 'Axios, where are we going?'

He alighted and held out his hand. I slid out of the car, still in a daze, and didn't resist when he pulled me close.

'You've lived in fear for over a year, while bearing and caring for our son. You've loved him unconditionally when you could've taken a different option without judgement. But you

don't need to be alone in this. You never need
to be alone again,' he vowed.

The depth of his words made my heart pound
with tentative hope. That hope turned to shock
when I spotted the middle-aged man standing at
the door of the plane.

'Dr Trudeau...what are you...? What's he
doing here?' I asked Ax.

'He's here to help. As are the others.'

Taking my hand, he led me onto the plane. And
my shock tripled.

'Mama?' Seated amongst three other distinguished-looking men was my mother. When she
smiled tremulously and held out her arms a broken sob ripped through me as I rushed forward
and threw myself into her embrace.

'Your husband rightly felt that you should be
surrounded by those you love in your time of
need.'

Did that include him?

Fearing I'd give myself away if I looked his
way, I kept my gaze on my mother.

'You should've told us, Callie.'

I shook my head. 'I couldn't risk not having
Andreos.'

And that seemed to settle the matter with her.
She nodded, then looked over my head. I didn't
need the signal to know that Ax was approaching.

'Let me introduce you, Calypso.'

Swiping my hand across my cheek, I composed myself and stood. Besides Dr Trudeau, the three men were all doctors too, specialising in everything to do with the cervix.

'Your mother has been instrumental in providing details about your grandmother's condition. With your permission, we'll head to Dr Trudeau's clinic and start the tests.'

I gasped, my gaze finding Ax's. 'That's what you've been doing the last three days? Rounding up specialists?'

He nodded, that blaze burning brighter in his eyes. 'You are far too important, *yineka mou*. I'm leaving nothing to chance.'

I swayed. He caught me, held me tight.

After pinning me with his gaze for several seconds, he glanced around. 'We're about to take off,' he said. 'I would like to talk to my wife in private, so I trust you can all amuse yourselves?' At their agreement, he turned to me. 'Calypso?'

I nodded, a million hopes and dreams cascading through my brain as I followed him into the master suite.

He waited long enough for me to be seated and buckled in before stalking over to the drinks cabinet. Dazedly, I watched him pour a glass of cognac, grimace, and pour a thimbleful into a second glass. Walking over, he handed the smaller drink to me.

'A small sip won't hurt,' he stated gruffly, almost pleadingly.

With another befuddled nod I accepted it, took the tiniest sip and shuddered my way through swallowing it down. As the spirit warmed my insides, another sensation filtered through. But the joy bubbling beneath my skin fizzled out when Axios sank onto his knees before me.

'Was it just about Andreos?' he asked starkly. 'Were you leaving only because of him or did I feature anywhere in your thoughts?'

'Ax—'

'I know I didn't give you the wedding of your dreams, or make the time after that palatable. But did I drive you away completely, Calypso?'

There was a layer of self-loathing in his voice that propelled me to grip his hand. 'I just didn't want to burden you—'

'Burden me? You're my *wife!*'

'One who was a stranger when we exchanged vows! I didn't know how…what you would do…'

'What I would *do*? What other option was there besides seeking medical—' His curse ranged through the room. 'Did you think I'd exploit you the way your father did your mother?'

'I didn't know then.'

For an eternity he simply stared at me. '*Then?* Does that mean you know different now?' he asked, his voice awash with hope and his eyes alight with a peculiar kind of desperation that tore through me.

I didn't realise my nails were digging into the sofa until he set his hand on mine, stilling my agitation. I wanted to cling to him. *Theos* did I want to. But the fear of fanning false hope, triggering another torrent of might-have-beens that would further shatter my heart, stopped me.

Discarding his drink, he took both my hands in his. 'Tell me, please, if I have a chance with you. No matter what happens I intend to stay and fight this thing along with you. But after that—'

I pressed a hand to his lips. 'We might not have a future,' I whispered. 'It wasn't just about Andreos. I didn't want to put *you* through that.'

His fingers tightened around mine, and when his eyes fused with mine, I felt the live wire of his desperation.

'That's why you tried to leave me again this time?'

Suspecting I wouldn't be able to speak around the lump in my throat, I nodded.

A hoarse breath shuddered out of him. 'I never thought I'd be so relieved at such a reason for being dumped.'

He stopped abruptly, caught my face between his hands and blazed me a look so intense my insides melted.

'I love you, Calypso. I fell in love with your defiance in Bora Bora. Fell in love with you when I saw your love for our son. I adored your strength when I watched that video. Watching you paint, seeing your talent…awed me. Despite the odds, you have fought and continue to fight for what you want. One day our son will grow up to learn what an inspiration you are. He'll watch you and know he has the best mother in the world.'

The tears came free and unchecked. 'Oh, Ax…'

'Getting the call that you'd gone the morning after our wedding altered something inside me. I wasn't ready to admit it, but I knew I'd failed you. That I'd failed myself. Your agreeing to take a leap with me felt like a second chance. And with every breath I vow to make it worth your while.'

'Was…was this what you were going to tell me in Thailand?'

'Yes. I knew I was in love with you. I planned on begging you to give our marriage a chance. But—'

'But I chopped you off at the knees before you could lay out everything my own heart and soul wanted to tell you. That I loved you and would've given anything to remain your wife.'

He froze. 'Say that again, please?' he begged.

'I love you, too, Ax. Even before the possibility of Andreos and the possibility of love I was drawn to you. Something inside me made me put *you* at the top of my bucket list. I was always going to come back, even if only for a short time, because my heart knew I belonged to you. And these last few weeks have felt like a heaven I didn't want to leave. I may have been devastated when you left me the morning after our wedding, but watching you leave me in Thailand…'

He closed his eyes for a single moment. 'I knew I was making a mistake even before I got on the helicopter after our wedding night. But when I left this time I knew I was coming straight back. That nothing would stop me. Because you're my heart, *pethi mou*. My very soul.'

To cement that vow he slanted his lips over mine, kissed me until we were both breathless.

'Tell me again,' I commanded.

His eyes burned with feeling. 'I love you. With all that I am and everything in between.'

He kissed me again as the plane sped down the runway and soared into the sky.

When I broke away to look out of the window, he gently caught my chin in his hand. 'What is it?'

'Andreos.'

A warm smile split Ax's face. 'He has Sophia and a dozen other staff curled around his plump little fingers. They will take care of him until we send for him in the morning. He's our little miracle and we will fight this thing together. All three of us. For now, you will let me take care of you. You will allow me the privilege of helping to make you better. Please, my love?'

I nodded, but still hesitated. 'What if it's too late? What if they can't…?'

He slid his thumb across my lips, silencing my doubts. 'Whatever happens we face it together. For better or worse, you have me for life. I will never leave your side and I will never fail you again.'

His words unfurled my joy. This time I wasn't alone. I had my precious baby and the husband of my heart. I intended to fight with everything I had for the chance to ensure my days were blessed with nothing but love, health and happiness.

At cruising altitude, Axios swung me into his arms and strolled to the bed. I curled my arms around his neck and looked into molten eyes blazing with love.

'I love you, Calypso,' he said again, as if saying the words filled him with as much happiness as it filled my heart.

'*Se agapo*, Axios.

EPILOGUE

A year later

'WHAT ARE YOU DOING?'

'Starting on your payback,' Axios drawled, striding across the master bedroom in Agistros to lay me down on the king-sized bed before trailing his lips over my shoulder to the sensitive area beneath my earlobe.

'What?' I gasped, delightful shivers running through me at the wickedness he evoked.

'You owe me a full pregnancy experience. I can't think of a better time to start than now. I want to experience it all—from morning sickness to the moment our baby enters the world.'

I made a face. 'Morning sickness isn't very sexy.'

He dropped a kiss on the corner of my mouth. 'Perhaps not. But I made you a promise to be here for the good as well as the bad, *eros mou.* So I will be on hand to hold your hair when you throw up. To massage your feet when the weight of our child tires you. And everything you need in between. If that's what you want too?' he asked, hope brimming in his voice.

I curled my arms around his neck. 'More than anything in the world.'

The operation to remove what had turned out to be a benign lump in my cervix six months ago had been a resounding success, with every trace of it gone and quarterly scans showing it hadn't returned.

Today Dr Trudeau had given us the all-clear to try for another baby—a statement Axios seemed determined to capitalise on immediately. And with a doting grandmother to help care for Andreos, in the form of my mother, life couldn't have been better. Her decision to leave my father hadn't been easy, but I'd supported her. Yiannis Petras hadn't resisted for long, busy as he was with frittering away his millions on one bad investment after another.

Ax groaned. 'Don't cry. It rips me up when you do.'

I laughed tremulously. 'Oh, God, then prepare yourself. Because I'm very hormonal during pregnancy.'

'Hmm, I will have to think of ways to counteract that.'

'What did you have in mind?'

'Why, endless seduction, of course. I can think

of nothing better than making love to my beautiful wife while she nurtures our baby in her womb.'

More tears flowed. With another groan, he sealed his lips to mine—most likely to distract me. It worked. Within minutes I was naked and gasping, lost in the arms of my true love.

And when, at the height of feeling, he looked deep into my eyes and whispered, 'I love you, Calypso,' he went one better and kissed my tears away.

The power of him moving inside me, possibly planting his seed inside me, triggered fresh tears.

I was still emotional when our breaths cooled. When he pulled me close and whispered in my ear.

'Our adventure is only just beginning, *eros mou*. And I couldn't have wished for a better partner at my side to experience it all but you, Calypso Xenakis.'

'Nor I, you, my love,' I returned, with every ounce of the love I held in my heart.

* * * * *

LET'S TALK
Romance

For exclusive extracts, competitions
and special offers, find us online:

 facebook.com/millsandboon

 @millsandboonuk

 @millsandboon

Or get in touch on 0844 844 1351*

For all the latest titles coming soon,
visit millsandboon.co.uk/nextmonth